Miss Pickerell
and the
War of the Computers

Miss Pickerell
and the
War of the Computers

by Dora Pantell

Series originated by Ellen MacGregor
Illustrated by Charles Geer

FRANKLIN WATTS
New York/London/Toronto/Sydney/1984

Library of Congress Cataloging in Publication Data

Pantell, Dora F.
Miss Pickerell and the war of the computers.
Summary: As supermarket prices begin rising mysteri-
ously, Miss Pickerell, attempting to solve the mystery,
finds herself caught in the middle of a war of the
computers.
1. Children's stories, American. [1. Mystery and
detective stories. 2. Supermarkets—Fiction. 3. Computers—Fiction] I. Title.
PZ7.P1934Mi 1984 [Fic] 84-7581
ISBN 0-531-04841-1

Contents

1
The Mystery in the Supermarket 1

2
Sampson Makes an Entrance 11

3
Computers That Talk to Each Other 19

4
Euphus Has His Say 29

5
"I Wouldn't Put Spying
Past Those Computers" 35

6
The Governor Agrees 45

7
Up on Bald Eagle Mountain 53

8
A Computer Called Homer 61

9
Who Did It, Homer? 73

10
Miss Pickerell Suspects 85

11
On the Villain's Trail 93

12
The House on the Mountaintop 103

13
Miss Pickerell Takes a Chance 111

14
A Perilous Journey 117

15
The Battle in the Sky 125

16
And Euphus Has the Last Word 129

IN MEMORY OF JOANNA,
THE CHILD WHOSE LOVE
MADE THE WORLD A BETTER PLACE
FOR ALL THE PEOPLE AND ANIMALS
WHO KNEW HER.

1

The Mystery in the Supermarket

Miss Pickerell settled her knitting bag and umbrella on the Square Toe City Supermarket checkout counter, pushed her eyeglasses another inch farther down on her nose, and peered over them to look at the numbers on the cash register. For one brief moment, she wondered whether she might not be losing her mind. She decided against it.

"It's all very odd!" she exclaimed, turning to her neighbor, Mrs. Broadribb, who stood on the checkout line behind her. "Those prices, I mean. Six cans of cat food, three in Tuna Surprise flavor and three in Savory Sonnet, should *not* cost $7.02."

Mrs. Broadribb inhaled and exhaled a very deep sigh. Her ample bosom heaved with the effort, and the bird-watching glasses that she wore around her neck bounced up and down on the purple-patterned blouse that she had on.

"Precisely my opinion," she replied. "I have just been saying as much to Mr. Trilling here. I have

1

also been telling him my objections to the fact that we have no other market nearby and . . ."

Mr. Trilling, Square Toe County's only piano tuner and Mrs. Broadribb's best friend, nodded his vigorous agreement.

"And," he added, not letting her finish her sentence, "I have been saying that the oddity of the prices, as you put it, Miss Pickerell, is easily explained. My experience with musical instruments has given me the clue."

Miss Pickerell could not exactly see the connection, but she did not want to be impolite. She made no comment.

"I have always advised my clients," Mr. Trilling went on, "not to have new keys put into an ancient piano. And for the same reason, I do not approve of the super-modern equipment this old market has just installed on its premises."

Miss Pickerell looked up and down and around the store to see to what equipment he was referring. She couldn't find a thing. Mr. Trilling waited for her puzzled glance to return to him.

"I am talking about *this*," he said, pointing with his chin at the dark strip of leather running the length of the checkout counter. "Of course, you probably did not notice it because . . ."

"For your information," Miss Pickerell broke in as soon as he paused to take a breath, "this conveyor belt was installed right after Thanksgiving last year. That was nearly eight months ago, and I noticed it then. I also . . ."

2

Mr. Trilling was not listening.

"Because," he repeated, "you may not be interested in computerized conveyor belts."

Miss Pickerell stopped talking and shuddered. If she ever heard the word *computer* again, she was afraid she would scream. Her seven nieces and nephews practically never spoke about anything else anymore. Her middle nephew, Euphus, the one who was so good in science, sometimes used words she couldn't find even in the latest edition of her encyclopedia. And her oldest niece, Rosemary, had announced only the other day that she was "into computers," too. She planned to become a computer analyst when she grew up. Miss Pickerell had no idea what a computer analyst was. She also had no intention of finding out. But she wasn't entirely certain that Mr. Trilling's opinion of the computerized conveyor belt was correct.

"As I was about to tell you, Mr. Trilling," she said, interrupting a statement he was now making about the dangers of a number of modern inventions, "I also discussed the subject of computerized conveyor belts with my middle nephew, Euphus. He stated that they were very fast, completely foolproof, and that they could be installed in the Square Toe City Supermarket without any problems at all."

Mr. Trilling, who had a habit of talking through very tight lips whenever his opinions were questioned, began to do so now.

"Your middle nephew, Euphus," he said, "does not know everything there is to know."

3

"What he said sounded very sensible to me," Miss Pickerell replied coldly. "He said that the belt had a bar code reader and . . ."

"A bar code *reader?*" Mrs. Broadribb interrupted, her eyebrows raised in disbelief.

"A bar code reader," Miss Pickerell repeated. "He explained it to me when I asked about the lines on the can. I asked Annie about them, too, but she didn't know."

Annie, the checkout girl, who was listening to every word in between quick glances around the empty store and much longer looks at the big clock fixed into the wall above the vegetable bin, said that she remembered.

"It was nearly closing time that day, too, Miss Pickerell," she said. "And you asked me what my mother and father were doing, now that they had moved out of their needlework shop to make way for the pizza parlor that was going to move in and pay more rent. And then you said that you were not at all sure that your cat would like the two Vegetable Stew flavors you were buying."

"He didn't," Miss Pickerell told her. "He gave me a very disgusted look after he finished sniffing at his saucer."

"Please continue about the bar code reader, Miss Pickerell," Mr. Trilling reminded her.

"I'll show you," Miss Pickerell said, holding up one of her Savory Sonnet cans and squinting at the six lines printed on the label. "Four of these are wide and two are narrow. The four lines are close together and the two are far apart. Different items

4

have different line arrangements. And that arrangement makes up a *code* that is machine readable."

Mr. Trilling was puckering up his mouth again. Miss Pickerell hastened to go on.

"There is a scanner in the conveyor belt," she said, pausing for a moment to make sure she was repeating Euphus's information correctly. "When the bar code passes over a tiny laser light in the conveyor belt, the scanner converts the code into the numbers that flash on the cash register display. And I disagree with you in any case about the super-modern equipment, Mr. Trilling, because the prices didn't change until today, so that . . ."

"Not today," Annie announced. "They changed on Wednesday."

"On Wednesday," Miss Pickerell murmured, counting the days off on her fingers. "That's nearly a week. I had no idea . . ."

"I know," Annie nodded. "Customers from up on Square Toe Mountain where you live don't come into the store that often. But practically nobody has been coming in lately. It will be even worse when they stop taking cash."

"Stop taking *cash?*" Mrs. Broadribb and Mr. Trilling gasped together.

"When they start the credit card system," Annie explained. "I'll just have to put the groceries into the bags then. I'll probably quit. I won't be able to stand the monotony."

Miss Pickerell could sympathize with Annie's sentiments. But she wished she would go on with the job, for now at least.

"If you will give me my change, Annie," she said, handing her a ten-dollar bill, "I would like to . . ."

"I understand," Annie said, smiling. "The animals are waiting outside in the trailer."

Miss Pickerell smiled back. She almost never went anywhere without her animals. Nancy Agatha, her cow, sat in the little trailer that was attached to the back of the automobile. The trailer had a red-fringed awning over it to protect the cow from bad weather. Pumpkins, the big black cat with the huge golden eyes, sometimes sat in the trailer with Nancy Agatha. Most of the time he sat on the front seat and looked out of the window. He was probably staring out of that window right now, Miss Pickerell reflected, and wondering what had happened to her.

"My change please, Annie," she said again.

But Annie hadn't quite finished talking.

"And our animal food customers!" she exclaimed. "Take poor old Mrs. Lonigan, for example. Her little dog, Sally—the brown one with the very short legs—is the only friend she has left. All Mrs. Lonigan's other friends are dead, and she has no relations. I know she'd rather starve than give Sally up, but . . ."

Miss Pickerell motioned frantically for Annie to stop. She couldn't bear to hear even one more word.

"I'd like to go now," she began again.

But Mr. Trilling hadn't completely finished with what he had to say, either. He lifted a Savory Sonnet can from the counter and held it up to the light.

"I see that there are some numbers on one side of the bar code," he commented. "These, I believe, are 764729."

Mrs. Broadribb, who was helping him look, first without her bird-watching glasses and then through them, added that she also saw the letters *Y* and *U* on the other side.

"I suppose Euphus explained all that, too," she said, sounding as though she were sure that he hadn't.

Miss Pickerell threw both her and Mr. Trilling an icy look.

"Certainly," she replied. "He said that the numbers and the letters are the *real* code."

"Not *another* code!" Mr. Trilling exclaimed sarcastically.

"Not another code," Miss Pickerell snapped. "The lines only *represent* the letters and numbers that are the real code."

"Why?" Mr. Trilling demanded.

"Because," Miss Pickerell replied, "the bar code only *identifies* the can of cat food or whatever the merchandise is. Then . . ."

Mrs. Broadribb and Mr. Trilling stood silent, waiting for her to continue.

Hoping against hope that she was not mixing it all up, she added, "Then the store's computer matches the item with the current price, which is supplied by the computer. And that price is correct unless . . ."

She hesitated. She really did not want to go on.

"Unless *what?*" Mr. Trilling insisted.

"Unless the computer has gone . . . has gone mad," she ended lamely.

Mr. Trilling and Mrs. Broadribb stared at her. Both of them had their mouths open. Then Mr. Trilling gulped. Mrs. Broadribb made an equally strange sound in her throat.

"But," Miss Pickerell stated quickly, "I'm not sure what Euphus really meant when he said that. He was halfway out my kitchen door, and he didn't want to answer any more questions."

Her own patience was wearing thin, too. She picked up the change that Annie had finally put on the checkout counter and began fitting the paper bag filled with cans into her already overstuffed knitting bag. Mr. Trilling and Mrs. Broadribb were still complaining, this time about the price of the three pounds of seedless grapes that Mrs. Broadribb was buying. Annie was telling them how the system worked with fruits.

"The scale is connected to the computer, too," she was saying. "Anyway, you could have figured it for yourself, if you'd looked at the prices stamped on the big plastic bags. Let's say that there are nine pounds of grapes in one of those bags. If you divide the price by nine to get the price of one pound and multiply by three, you . . ."

Mr. Trilling cut her short.

"Never mind all that," he said. "Tell me instead why grapes should cost so much to begin with. This has been a very good year for them everywhere they grow. There have been no droughts, no floods, no . . ."

Miss Pickerell left them to their arguing. She pushed a hairpin that had come loose firmly back under her hat, picked up her knitting bag and her umbrella, and walked out into the pale sunshine of a fading summer day. It was still quite warm, but she shivered as she made her way to the corner where she had parked her automobile and trailer. She couldn't get the picture of poor old Mrs. Lonigan and Sally out of her mind. And she actually had no idea as to just what Euphus had meant when he said what he did about computers going mad.

"I must ask him about that," she whispered, as she interrupted her walking for a second to button up her sweater. "I really *must!*"

2

Sampson Makes an Entrance

It was not until she had apologized to Pumpkins and Nancy Agatha for leaving them alone for so long, and was sitting in her automobile with her engine throbbing, that Miss Pickerell saw the black and white dog with the floppy ears. He was half hidden by the pots of high laurel bushes that Mr. Stotz, Sr., and Mr. Stotz, Jr., owners of the new pizza parlor, had put out on the sidewalk. Mr. Stotz, Sr., called the pots a voluntary public service. Miss Pickerell knew better. She was a member of the Citizens' Committee that had complained to the Mayor and then to her friend, the Governor, about the condition of that particular sidewalk. And she strongly suspected that he, Mr. Stotz, Sr., had gotten the pots so that he could sweep the litter under them. She often promised herself that she would someday make a *thorough* inspection of exactly what was going on under those pots.

But she didn't stop to do this now. She jammed on her brakes and took another look at the dog. He was tied by a coarse rope to a stick pushed into the middle of one of the bushes. The other end of the rope was knotted tightly around his neck.

"Forevermore!" Miss Pickerell whispered. "That thick rope must be choking him! And what is that piece of paper dangling from the rope?"

She sighed heavily as she got out of the automobile.

"I'd better go and see," she told herself. "If I don't do it now, I know I'll only turn around and come back ten minutes later."

The dog made a small, grateful sound when Miss Pickerell loosened the knot. He stood very still while she stroked his head with one hand and tore the piece of paper away from the rope with the other. There were three lines of printing in large black letters on the paper. Miss Pickerell read them with mounting horror.

"His name is Sampson," the note stated. "And he's a good dog. He loves bones and canned dog food. But my mother says he eats too much, and we don't have enough money to feed him."

"Oh, no!" Miss Pickerell gasped. "It can't be true!!"

But it was. And Sampson was looking hopefully up at her. Miss Pickerell tried hard to ignore the look.

"Impossible!" she told him, while she stared straight ahead. "I can't, I simply can't pick up every stray animal that I meet. I can't even take you to

12

the Animal Shelter. They already have a long waiting list. And I certainly can't put you into the Home for Aged and Retired Animals. In the first place, you're not eligible. In the second place, they have no room, either. On the other hand, I *can't* just leave you here . . ."

She was still debating the problem when she felt something cold and wet at her ankles. It was Sampson waiting for her decision.

"Oh, all right," she said weakly. "Come on!"

Nancy Agatha flatly refused to move over when Miss Pickerell led Sampson into the trailer. Pumpkins arched his back and hissed.

"I know, I know," Miss Pickerell said to Nancy Agatha, as she leaned over to give her cow a gentle pat. "He's not your friend yet. And I know what you want, Pumpkins. You want to sit on my lap, right?"

Pumpkins purred when Miss Pickerell got into the car and settled him in his favorite place. He looked down his nose at Sampson, crouching timidly in the seat beside him. Miss Pickerell breathed a sigh of relief as she put the key in the ignition, and began driving out of Square Toe City.

"Well, that's settled," she told herself while she drove past the Square Toe City post office and the Main Street coffee shop and the new beauty parlor where her oldest niece, Rosemary, had told her how they used only blowers to style their customers' hair. Miss Pickerell had meant to ask Rosemary where those customers went who wanted their hair set with clips or rollers in the regular way. But she had never

13

gotten around to her question. And she was certainly not going to spend any time wondering about it now. She was much too worried.

"This is only the beginning," she remarked to Pumpkins, as she reached the end of Main Street and made the turn onto the highway. "This heartless abandoning of animals! Or maybe the people are plain desperate and are just as miserable as the animals they're abandoning. Either way, with prices what they are, there'll be dozens of homeless animals left to starve in the streets. And, as I said, I *can't* take them *all.*"

Pumpkins meowed his approval of Miss Pickerell's last statement. But he added his disapproval when two drivers behind Miss Pickerell honked for her to get out of the way.

"I have never driven my automobile more than thirty-five miles an hour," Miss Pickerell called out her window to the drivers, "and I don't intend to start now. I do *not* believe in reckless driving. Besides, I'm in the slow lane."

The drivers continued to honk. One of them shouted at her when she finally turned off the highway and onto the road that went up the mountain. Miss Pickerell paid no attention. She straightened her hat, which had fallen to one side when she was calling out to the drivers, and thought again about computers.

"They're taking over the world. That's what those machines are doing," she complained. "I wouldn't be too surprised if even those birds you're listening to, Pumpkins, weren't chattering about them this very minute. The squirrels, too!"

She felt better about the bird population, though, when she looked up into the trees and saw a fat mother robin sitting on one of the branches, surrounded by her babies. She seemed to be giving them some sort of command and waiting for them to obey. When they didn't, she repeated her speech. Then, after scratching her head for a second, she gently nudged the baby nearest her off the branch.

"She's teaching her children how to fly!" Miss Pickerell exclaimed happily. "She certainly doesn't have *her* mind on any computers."

The sight of the brilliant copper birches and the red maple trees lining the sides of the private road leading up to her farm made Miss Pickerell feel even better. When she approached her lawn, full of the fluffy pink, blue, and white Michaelmas daisies she had planted in the spring, she felt better still. And when she drove past her kitchen garden on her way to the barn and inhaled the fresh scent of the parsley, thyme, and mint growing brightly in their own corner, she came close to forgetting about computers. She settled Nancy Agatha in the barn and, with Pumpkins racing ahead and Sampson close behind, ran back across the garden and up the wooden steps to her kitchen. Pumpkins, meowing lustily, rushed to sit in front of the shining white cabinet where Miss Pickerell kept his cans of cat food.

"Yes, yes," she assured him, as she hastily placed her hat, umbrella, and knitting bag on the

15

stool underneath the black wall telephone. "It's nearly seven o'clock, and you're very hungry."

Sampson was even hungrier than Pumpkins. Miss Pickerell wondered when he had eaten last, as she watched him gulp down some of the chicken she had prepared for her own supper. Pumpkins waited politely for him to finish before starting on the Savory Sonnet that Miss Pickerell put in his bowl. He had licked the bowl clean by the time Miss Pickerell sat down at her kitchen table to drink a cup of tea.

"I'm much too tired to have anything more," she said to herself. "Too tired and too worried! What *is* going to happen to all those other hungry animals? To little Sally, for example? And to poor old Mrs. Lonigan, who loves her so much?"

Neither Pumpkins nor Sampson replied. Pumpkins had jumped up on the kitchen windowsill, where he sat among the geranium plants, giving himself a careful face wash. Sampson lay stretched out on the plastic mat with the words PET CAFETERIA on it. Every once in a while, he raised his head to look gratefully at Miss Pickerell. Then he lapped up some of the fresh water she had put out for him, breathed a long, contented sigh, and went to sleep. Miss Pickerell wished she could feel as comfortable as he did.

"But I don't," she said out loud, as she paced up and down the linoleum-covered kitchen floor that she had mopped and polished just before she left for the supermarket. "And I'm getting dizzier and dizzier looking at these linoleum squares."

She moved into the little hall at the far end of

the kitchen and began a new march. The third time around, she decided to rest for a while on the narrow horsehair sofa that stood against the left-hand wall.

"It could clear my head and help me to *think*," she told herself encouragingly. "I'll concentrate on what Euphus said about computers going mad. That, I believe, is the main problem."

But no thoughts came into her head. And she kept tossing from one side to the other on the horsehair sofa.

"I suppose I'm too upset to rest," she sighed. "Maybe I should count sheep. People say that's very relaxing. I don't know enough sheep to count, though. Maybe I ought to count my blessings, instead."

At the moment, Miss Pickerell couldn't think of too many blessings, either. She decided to count the roses on the flower-patterned carpet next to the horsehair sofa. She was up to rose number 19 when she saw a hole in the carpet she had never noticed before. It was a small hole, and it could probably be patched with some of the wool she had in her attic. Red to match the roses or pink to go with the places between the roses would be best. Trying hard to decide just which color would be less noticeable as a small patch on the carpet, Miss Pickerell fell fast asleep.

3

Computers That Talk to Each Other

It was Sampson who woke her from her sleep. Somebody was knocking at the kitchen door, and Sampson, barking at the top of his lungs, wanted Miss Pickerell to know about it. She opened her eyes to sunlight streaming in through the kitchen window right into the little hall where she lay.

"Good heavens!" she exclaimed. "I've been on this hard horsehair sofa all night. I never even got out of my clothes or took my glasses off. It's a wonder the glasses didn't break. I guess I didn't move around very much."

The knocking at the door continued. So did Sampson's barking.

"All right, all right," she called out, as she smoothed her skirt and ran to the door. "I'm coming!"

Euphus, carrying a box wrapped in stiff brown paper with a large number of stamps on the front, was standing outside. He raced into the kitchen and sat down at the table. He shook his head when Miss Pickerell asked him if he wanted something to eat.

"This just came in the mail," he told her, pointing to the box he had placed on the table. "Wait till I show you!"

Miss Pickerell did not pay very much attention. She had too much to think about at the moment to wonder about her middle nephew's mail. Euphus was always writing away to scientists somewhere and getting all sorts of packages back. She was even less interested than usual right now because she was busy organizing in her mind the various questions she wanted to ask him. She was also hoping that he would answer in a way that made some sense. Euphus had no intention of keeping quiet about his box, however.

"Look, Aunt Lavinia," he shouted. "Look what I won in the interschool science competition. A portable computer!"

Miss Pickerell shuddered instantly. She felt very proud of her middle nephew, Euphus. And she was certainly planning to let Mr. Trilling and Mrs. Broadribb know about this new science victory of his. She just *wished* the prize had not been a computer.

"That's very nice," she said as calmly as she could, while she took a quick look at the small computer screen and keyboard he was happily pointing out to her and then gazed unbelievingly at Euphus. He seemed to have grown an inch since she had seen him last week. His mother, she noticed, had already let down the cuffs of the navy blue shorts he was wearing. And Euphus had complained, when his mother had bought them for him only a month ago, that they were "way too big."

"It's OK," he was saying now. "I mean it's a pretty good machine. It can play chess with me. It'll be a better partner than Rosemary. She's very lazy about chess. She's lazy about a lot of other things, too."

Miss Pickerell did not ask him what other things he had in mind. She was too occupied with Pumpkins and Sampson.

"Just a minute! Just a minute!" she was pleading with them. "I'm getting your breakfast as fast as I can."

Pumpkins gobbled up the food Miss Pickerell put in his saucer and joined Sampson at his plate. Sampson growled once, then wagged his tail.

"Whose dog is that, anyway?" Euphus asked. "I've never seen him before."

"He's mine now," Miss Pickerell said briefly. "I found him. His name is Sampson."

Euphus bent down to pet him. Sampson reached up to give Euphus a return lick on the nose.

"I think he wants to go out now, Aunt Lavinia," Euphus stated. "He's asking me to open the door."

"We're all going out now," Miss Pickerell replied. "I haven't milked Nancy Agatha yet. Or taken her to the pasture."

Euphus ran alongside of Miss Pickerell as she practically galloped across the kitchen garden to the barn. He said nothing while Miss Pickerell milked her cow and murmured comforting words to her. But when they left the barn and started walking up to the pasture, he told Miss Pickerell that he had an idea.

"I've been thinking," he said slowly, "I've been thinking about that dog of yours. I've decided that what you need for him is a computer."

Miss Pickerell stopped in the middle of a step she was taking to stare at him.

"I've been thinking, too," she said. "What I have decided is that I can't imagine anything I need *less*."

"But you don't understand," Euphus insisted when they started walking again. "I said it was for *Sampson*. You see, if you had a computer you could program it to let him in and out of the house. You'd need to hook up the computer to an electronic sensor, which could control a latch that would open and close the door. And there'd be a tape to call out the dog's name. Just imagine that, Aunt Lavinia!"

"I don't see why I should," Miss Pickerell said, "since I have no trouble in letting Sampson in and out by myself."

Euphus gave her a very scornful look.

"I'm talking about when you're *not* home," he explained. "A lot of things can happen when you're away from the house. A pipe can burst, for example, and cause a flood."

"Heaven forfend!" Miss Pickerell whispered, while she led Nancy Agatha to the grassiest part of the pasture, told her she would come back to visit her later, and hurried down the hill again.

"You can program the computer to notify a plumber for just such an emergency," Euphus continued, as he hurried after her. "Did you know that, Aunt Lavinia? I can give you all the details, if you like. Anytime."

"Not at the moment, thank you, Euphus," Miss Pickerell replied, panting a little as she reentered her kitchen. "Right now, I'm going upstairs to bathe and change my clothes."

Euphus looked puzzled. Miss Pickerell didn't bother to explain.

"What I want you to do while I'm changing," she said to him, "is to write down some scientific information. Will you do that, Euphus?"

"Sure," Euphus told her. "Should I draw some diagrams, too?"

Miss Pickerell sighed. She knew how impossible it was to understand some of Euphus's diagrams.

"Only if they fit in with your information," she answered. "I want you to write down EVERYTHING you know about computer codes and *exactly* what you meant the other day when you talked about a computer going mad."

She handed him the ballpoint pen that she kept clipped to her reminder pad near the telephone and told him he would find a pad of yellow lined paper on the desk in the parlor.

Euphus nodded.

"But I should tell you," he said, when she started climbing the narrow flight of stairs that led from the little hall up to the second floor of her house, "I really should mention, Aunt Lavinia, that if you had a computer, it could also run your bath water for you."

Miss Pickerell groaned her answer. She groaned still more desperately when she heard singing coming from the parlor television set that Euphus had turned on. It was so loud, she could hear it even over the water running into her tub.

Euphus was gone by the time she came downstairs again. He had not used the pad of yellow paper she had suggested. He had written his notes on the back of a dry cleaner's bill that was lying on the kitchen table. It was all in the form of a list. Miss Pickerell gave her eyeglasses a thorough cleaning with her large white handkerchief and sat down to read the list.

1. THE COMPUTER ACCEPTS AND STORES INFORMATION IN ITS MEMORY. IT CAN BE PROGRAMMED TO PROCESS THAT INFORMATION.

2. PROCESSING INSTRUCTIONS CAN COME FROM A CENTRAL PLACE BY TELEPHONE. THERE IS AN ATTACHMENT WITH AN AUDIOTRANSMITTER OR COUPLER. INSTRUCTIONS CAN EVEN BE SENT THOUSANDS OF MILES ALONG GEOSYNCHRONOUS (STATIONARY) SATELLITE LINKS. THESE SATELLITES....

Miss Pickerell decided to skip the rest of this part for the moment. She also decided to postpone trying to figure out the small diagram that accompanied it. She went down the list to the next point:

3. COMPUTERS CAN GO MAD? DID I SAY THAT? WOW!!

Miss Pickerell read this part twice. She breathed a sigh of relief before she continued with the rest of the list:

4. COMPUTERS CAN BE CONNECTED TO TALK TO EACH OTHER OVER THE TELEPHONE. ISN'T THAT SOMETHING? MAYBE THAT'S WHEN THEY GO MAD, WHEN THEY FIGHT WITH EACH OTHER.
5. I HAVE TO LEAVE NOW. I LIKE YOUR DOG.

YOUR LOVING NEPHEW,
EUPHUS

Miss Pickerell sat still for a while trying to imagine what computers could possibly have to say to each other or argue about, over the telephone or anywhere else. She got up when Pumpkins meowed his complaint about the dreadful television music that was disturbing his windowsill nap. Sampson, standing bolt upright at her feet, voiced his protest by yowling along with the singer.

"Yes," Miss Pickerell told them, "I think it's unbearable, too."

She was just walking into her parlor to turn the television set off when the singing came to a sudden stop. A voice announced, "We interrupt this program for an important message from our Mayor. Ladies and gentlemen, His Honor, the Mayor."

The Mayor, Miss Pickerell observed when his face appeared on the screen, was beginning to lose his hair. There was definitely a bald place on the top of his head, and he was trying to hide it by combing the rest of his hair straight back. It didn't help, Miss Pickerell decided.

As always, the Mayor began his television address by smiling broadly and saying, "Good morning, folks. I hope you are all feeling as fit as a fiddle." But his smile faded when he went on speaking.

"A number of worthy residents in Square Toe City," he said, "have brought the recent price crisis to my attention. This is a terrible thing that is happening, and I won't sit idly by and let it go on."

Applause from the studio audience interrupted the speech. The Mayor waved the appreciative clapping aside.

"We must act quickly to learn why this is happening and do something about it," he continued. "As a first step, I am calling for an open Council meeting at City Hall. I am scheduling it for 12:30

26

this afternoon. It is the only free time that I have, and it is also lunchtime for most people with jobs. If they like, they can bring along something to eat."

The Mayor's face disappeared from the screen. The blaring music came on again. Miss Pickerell quickly pressed the button that shut off the television set.

"A City Council meeting!" Miss Pickerell snorted, on her way back into the kitchen. "When I went to the last one, I promised myself *never* to go to another. And with very good reason!"

But as she prepared some breakfast for herself and told Pumpkins and Sampson, who were watching her hopefully, that they couldn't possibly be hungry again, she began to have some doubts about her decision. She had more and more doubts the longer she thought about it.

"No," she said, when she finally sat down at the table and started buttering the toast she had prepared to eat with her crisp cheese omelet. "There have been a number of Council meetings that I deliberately stayed away from. But I have ABSO-LUTELY no intention of missing *this* one!"

4

Euphus Has His Say

Miss Pickerell was a little late getting to the meeting. She had stopped in the Square Toe Precious Pet Shop on her way, to buy a collar for Sampson. Then she had driven another block to the Animal Shelter, to get him a dog license. When she finally got to City Hall, she couldn't find a parking space. She drove around and around the lot next to the City Council room where she wanted to park. She could keep an eye on her animals from the windows there. And she became angrier and angrier every time she drove around and saw the long green and white car that was parked at an angle. Its right wheel extended a good few inches into the empty space beside it.

"If it weren't for that car sticking out," she muttered the fourth time she passed it, "I'd have no problem moving into that space."

The fifth time she decided she'd had enough.

"If the person who owns that shiny and very

expensive vehicle can do it," she said to herself, "so can I!"

She squeezed most of her automobile and trailer into the reduced space. The part that didn't get in was distinctly blocking any exit for the small gray car on the other side. She came to terms with that issue, too.

"Unless this meeting turns out to be a whole lot different from some of the others I've attended," she told herself, "I will definitely be the first one to leave."

She waved to Nancy Agatha, Pumpkins, and Sampson and marched briskly up the broad white City Hall steps. At the top she turned right to walk past the Mayor's office and into the room with the sign CITY COUNCIL printed on the door.

The place was packed with people and buzzing with talk. Everybody in Square Toe County seemed to be there. The Mayor, in his shirtsleeves, stood on the dais, behind a table holding a glass, a pitcher of water, a wooden gavel, and a small, silver-colored bell. The rest of the room was full of uncomfortable-looking metal folding chairs lined up in rows. Euphus and Rosemary, Miss Pickerell noticed immediately, were in the very first row with Miss Ogelthorpe, the *Square Toe Gazette's* star reporter, sitting between them. Miss Ogelthorpe was holding a pencil in her hand and balancing an open notebook on her knees. The Mayor had not yet said a word, but Miss Ogelthorpe was already writing. Miss Pickerell supposed she was writing something about the attendance at the meeting. Euphus and Rosemary would know for sure. They were peering down into her notebook, one on each side of her, reading whatever she had written there.

Miss Pickerell found a chair in the third row, very near a window overlooking the parking lot. She looked out at Nancy Agatha, Pumpkins, and Sampson before she sat down. She smiled when she saw that they were all three being very friendly in the trailer and settled herself as comfortably as she could in the metal folding chair. Mr. Rugby, owner of the SQUARE TOE CITY DINER, MOONBURGERS OUR SPECIALTY, looking stouter than ever, sat on her left. Her friend, Professor Humwhistel, Square Toe City's leading scientist, wearing his usual old-fashioned vest with the gold watch chain dangling from the pocket, was on her right. Mr. Trilling and Mrs. Broadribb were in the row ahead. They turned around to say good morning to Miss Pickerell. Mr. Kettelson, the hardware store man who loved animals and especially adored Nancy Agatha and Pumpkins, leaned forward from the row behind to ask about Sampson. Miss Lemon, Square Toe County's chief telephone operator, sitting next to him, grew very red in the face when he mentioned the dog.

"Euphus was telephoning all his friends about Sampson," she apologized between blushes. "I really didn't think you'd mind, Miss Pickerell, if I mentioned it to Mr. Kettelson and to Professor Humwhistel here and . . ."

Miss Pickerell was about to discuss this with her when she noticed how everybody was looking up at the dais. The Mayor was trying to call the

31

meeting to order. He rapped on the table with the wooden gavel and rang the silver-colored bell a number of times. Then he cleared his throat.

"Ladies and gentlemen," he shouted, "if we want to address this question of unexplained high prices, we'd better start right now. We don't have much time and . . ."

"We certainly *do* want to address this question of UNBELIEVABLY high prices," Mrs. Broadribb interrupted. "And I suggest that we begin by organizing a picket line to march around City Hall."

Scattered applause greeted Mrs. Broadribb's recommendation.

"But that's ridiculous!" Mr. Kettelson shouted above the applause. "It was our Mayor at City Hall who called this meeting. Why should we picket *him?*"

The applause died down. The Mayor beamed at Mr. Kettelson.

Miss Lemon got up to say that she knew for a *fact* that the baby hospital on the corner of Main Street and Mulberry Lane was desperate because it couldn't afford to buy the baby food it needed at the new prices. She also knew for a fact that the people in nearby Plentibush City were getting ready to riot about the prices. They had even drawn up a riot plan.

The Mayor did not bother to ask Miss Lemon where she had gotten her information. Everybody in and around Square Toe City knew that Miss Lemon listened in on telephone conversations. But Miss Lemon began to offer Miss Pickerell her excuse.

"I couldn't *help* overhearing," she whispered. "When the Mayor and the Governor were talking, I mean. They were so excited that they were actually screaming. I would have had to wear earplugs not to hear what they were saying."

Miss Pickerell did not answer. She was listening to Mr. Wolin, who ran the shoemaker shop on Sunningdale Avenue. He was saying thât, in his opinion, it was all due to inflation. Mr. Walker, who owned the rival shoemaker shop on Walnut Street, rose instantly to correct him. Inflation was nowhere near as high as the new prices, he wanted Mr. Wolin to know. Inflation could not possibly be the cause.

A man in the back of the room, whom Miss Pickerell did not recognize, said that the constantly changing value of the American dollar might have something to do with the prices. This point of view was instantly contradicted by the Square Toe City librarian, who gave full details to prove her opinion. The meeting droned on and on. Nobody said anything that gave any hint of a solution.

The Mayor took a long look at his watch, sipped some water from his glass, and rapped again with his gavel.

"I am setting up a number of committees for further intensive study," he said. "The rise in prices could be due to any of the causes you wonderful people brought up at this meeting. It could also be due to . . ."

"To computers!" a voice screeched from the front of the room. "The computers could be warring with each other and doing something weird to the price calculations!"

It was Euphus, standing on his chair to make sure that the Mayor could hear what he was saying. The Mayor stared at him. Everybody else laughed.

"Isn't it just like Euphus to think of such a thing!" Miss Pickerell heard Mrs. Broadribb comment.

Mr. Trilling agreed with her. So did the three ladies from the Why Not Knit It department in the Square Toe City General Store. They said he was a very nice child, but that he was surely watching too many science fiction movies.

Chairs scraped as the meeting broke up. Miss Pickerell, making her way to the door, commented to Professor Humwhistel that it had been a total waste of time.

"Nobody said a word that amounted to anything," she told him. "And I don't think they should have laughed at Euphus. In my opinion, his idea about a war between computers made as much sense as any of the other silly suggestions that some of those people came up with."

Professor Humwhistel puffed on his half-empty pipe and looked down at her thoughtfully.

"Perhaps even much more sense, Miss Pickerell," he said very quietly.

5

"I Wouldn't Put Spying Past Those Computers"

Miss Pickerell could hardly believe her ears. She also had some difficulty in finding her voice.

"You . . . you mean that . . . ?" she stammered.

"Yes," Professor Humwhistel replied, while he steered her courteously through the crowds at the door and walked down the City Hall steps with her. "Yes, I do mean that there may be something in Euphus's suggestion. What those three dear ladies referred to as science fiction often has a sound scientific idea in it somewhere. And to some people at least, science often seems more like science fiction."

"I know just what you're describing, Professor," Miss Pickerell told him. "I sometimes think about it when I am on the telephone. That is, I think about a voice traveling thousands of miles across the land. Across oceans, too."

"We needn't go back to the invention of the telephone," Professor Humwhistel laughed, as they reached the bottom step and began walking toward

the parking lot. "Recent progress has been even more dramatic. Think of modern spaceships, for example, the way they rise up above the earth's atmosphere and travel to the moon, where you have already been and where you met Mr. Rugby in the moon cafeteria and . . ."

"Excuse me, Professor," Miss Pickerell interrupted. "But we are getting away from the subject. We were talking about what Euphus said at the meeting. The idea of computers warring with each other."

Professor Humwhistel was unfastening the two top buttons of his vest. It was a very hot day.

"Well," he said when he finished. "Euphus may have been oversimplifying. But it is perfectly true that new data can be fed into a computer to replace information that is already there. This can even be done over the telephone. People sometimes call it an overriding process."

Miss Pickerell was glad that they had reached the trailer and she could stop and talk to Nancy Agatha, Pumpkins, and Sampson. Her head was practically swimming with all this strange information.

"An overriding process?" she repeated.

Professor Humwhistel smiled.

"What that means," he said, "is that one set of computer instructions—a program—can replace another set of instructions in the computer's memory. Program #1 in the computer's memory, for example, might tell the computer to answer a question about whether the earth is revolving on its axis

37

with the word YES. Program #2 could change the instructions and put into the memory the answer NO, which is false, of course. The computer's memory bank consists only of the data that has been fed into it."

"I understand that part," Miss Pickerell nodded. "And the part about the telephone?"

"That's the easiest part of all," Professor Humwhistel told her. "Individual computers are simply plugged into a central computer through a telephone network. Computer instructions or other data go out over this network to computers that are connected to it."

"But how do they actually *talk* to each other?" Miss Pickerell asked, her mind still occupied with what Euphus had said about computer arguments.

"Typewritten instructions to the computer, which are stored as electronic impulses inside the computer, are converted into audible tones—sounds—that can be transmitted by an ordinary telephone," Professor Humwhistel explained.

Miss Pickerell frowned. All of this was extremely interesting, but she did not see what any of it had to do with the Square Toe City Supermarket and the way its prices were going up. She said as much to Professor Humwhistel.

"I am getting to that," Professor Humwhistel replied. "And I will . . ."

A commotion at the top of the stairs interrupted whatever else he was going to say. Mr. Rugby, now wearing the starched chef's hat he had taken off during the meeting, was pointing to his truck and trying to get past the people in front of him. Mr. Trilling, whom he had elbowed out of the way, was calling after him angrily. Mrs. Broadribb was trying to calm Mr. Trilling down while, at the same time, signaling with her hand for Miss Pickerell to wait. Miss Pickerell climbed into her automobile immediately. Professor Humwhistel jumped in beside her.

"We can go to my office to talk," he said quickly. "Or to Mr. Rugby's diner."

Miss Pickerell chose the diner. It was nearer.

Mr. Rugby was already dressed in his favorite apron, the one that was much too long for him, when they got to the diner. As always, he beamed when he saw Miss Pickerell and insisted that she and Professor Humwhistel sit at the middle table, which had the best waiter.

"And you needn't worry about not being near a window, Miss Pickerell," he added. "I will keep an eye on your animals for you."

"Not the center table today, thank you, Mr. Rugby," Miss Pickerell told him. "We would like a quiet table in the back."

"Certainly, certainly," he replied. "I have just the place for you. A booth for two. And I will wait on you personally."

He escorted them to the small booth in the rear of the restaurant, flipped his clean white towel over the purple, plush-lined seats to make sure there was not even a speck of dust on them, and stood ready with his order pad.

Miss Pickerell said that all she wanted was a peppermintade.

"Ah, yes," Mr. Rugby said approvingly. "Your favorite drink!"

Professor Humwhistel ordered some iced tea.

"A most refreshing beverage!" Mr. Rugby exclaimed. "And you shall have it in less time than it takes to . . ."

He finished his sentence on the way to the kitchen. Miss Pickerell waited only for him to be out of earshot.

"Yes, Professor?" she asked. "Please go on. You were about to tell me the connection between the Square Toe City Supermarket and the computer's memory bank."

"Right, the Square Toe City Supermarket," Professor Humwhistel repeated slowly, while he searched in his right-hand jacket pocket for the matches he was always losing. "You probably know, Miss Pickerell, that this market is part of a statewide chain, and like most large organizations these days, it works with the help of computers."

"I know it has a computerized conveyor belt near the cash register," Miss Pickerell replied promptly, "and that the latest prices are inside the computer. I learned about it from Euphus. He also told me that there was a scanner in the conveyor belt that converts the bar code into numbers that are then matched up with the prices in the computer."

"Euphus gave you the correct information," Professor Humwhistel stated. "What he may not have told you is that . . ."

40

Mr. Rugby, wheezing a little with the burden of the tray he carried in his hands, was approaching again.

"A peppermintade for Miss Pickerell," he announced, placing it with a flourish on the table before her. "And a glass of iced tea for the professor. And two Eclipse Specials—sponge cake and whipped cream topping made fresh this morning. In case you change your minds about eating something."

He bowed to both of them before he left. Miss Pickerell returned to the subject of computers.

"What was it you were saying, Professor," she asked, "about something Euphus might not have told me?"

Professor Humwhistel was staring into his iced tea. He seemed reluctant about going on.

"I hope I am not going to frighten you with this information," he said finally.

"I . . . I'm not frightened of most things," Miss Pickerell replied, trying to reassure herself as well as the professor.

"We all know that," Professor Humwhistel said, smiling. "And I will proceed. The Square Toe City Supermarket undoubtedly receives it prices from the Processing Center that sends them out over its telephone network to all the branch stores. First, of course, the programmer feeds any changes in price into the computer. What I mean is that the programmer instructs the computer to adjust the price code. The adjustment can be the addition of 1 percent on fruits and vegetables, for example, to cover higher farm prices, or a 2 percent discount for all large orders, and so on. These are general instructions which make it unnecessary for the programmer to feed the individual prices on each item into the computer.

"It all sounds very sensible to me," Miss Pickerell commented. "And when the market receives the latest price data, it stamps the prices on all the boxes and cans and bags—for the customer's information mostly. Please continue, Professor."

Professor Humwhistel was now searching in his left-hand pocket for his matches. Then he changed his mind and took a sip of his iced tea.

"If somebody has illegally broken into and altered the pricing program inside the computer, either by feeding new information in over the telephone or in some other way, then . . ."

"Then," Miss Pickerell breathed, "the prices will come out different from what they should be. And the merchandise will sell for incorrect prices."

"Quite so," Professor Humwhistel agreed sadly. "A person who gains illegal entry to the computer and the program can easily give orders for an incorrect change in price codes. The procedure resembles the example I gave you before, the one about the world turning on its . . ."

"I understand," Miss Pickerell burst out. "I understand what you are saying. But I don't believe for one moment that anyone would do such a terrible thing!"

"What do you believe?" the professor asked.

Miss Pickerell hesitated for only an instant.

"That the computers have gone mad," she said.

"Completely mad! That's another thing that Euphus said. Not at the meeting. He told that to me."

Professor Humwhistel gave her a very doubtful look.

"Stranger things have happened, I suppose," he sighed. "Personally, I don't believe it. On the other hand, I am not sure about my idea, either. I don't know who would be feeding the wrong prices into the computers or even *if* any such person is doing it. And I certainly don't know why!"

"Then we must find out," Miss Pickerell said decisively. "The first step is to decode the codes. Or is that the wrong way to say it? What I mean is, we have to find out what the price codes are saying to the bar codes."

"It is certainly a logical way to start," Professor Humwhistel replied, as he finally took some matches out of one of his pockets. "Unfortunately, I cannot help you in this respect. Computer programs are often kept secret. And I wouldn't know how to decipher the program even if it weren't kept secret."

"SECRET!" Miss Pickerell exploded. "Secret when the lives of people and animals are at stake? When the baby hospital has no money to buy the food it needs? When Mrs. Lonigan may have to give up her Sally? When the little boy or little girl who had to put Sampson out on the street is crying his or her heart out? When . . ."

Professor Humwhistel was no longer listening. He was looking off somewhere and thoughtfully nodding his head.

"The Supreme Court once said something like

what you are saying about secrets," he commented finally. "I believe the exact words were, THERE CAN BE NO SECRECY WHEN THE PUBLIC IS IN DANGER. The reference may have been to dangers from spies or . . ."

"I wouldn't put spying past those computers," Miss Pickerell interrupted. "I will make certain to explain that to the Processing Center."

"You can't . . ." Professor Humwhistel began.

"Pooh!" Miss Pickerell exclaimed indignantly. "Who is going to stop me? I have every right to express my opinion."

"You certainly have that right," the professor assured her. "But you cannot ask the Processing Center for access to the program. You need official permission for that."

"Then I will get that official permission," Miss Pickerell retorted.

She took a deep breath. She knew she was doing the right thing. And *nobody* was going to stop her.

"Yes," she said again, as she resolutely picked up her knitting bag and her umbrella. "I will most definitely get that official permission!!"

6

The Governor Agrees

The first thing Miss Pickerell did when she got back to her farm, even before she took Nancy Agatha out of the trailer and up to her pasture, was to telephone the Governor. Her call was picked up after the second ring. A cheerful voice announced, "Governor's Mansion" and, before Miss Pickerell could say even one word, proceeded to sing the state song. The singing was accompanied by a piano tinkling in the background.

"Forevermore!" Miss Pickerell breathed. "What will they think of next?"

She did not like to interrupt. But she made sure to begin talking the instant she heard the closing notes of the song.

"This is Miss Pickerell," she said, "Miss Pickerell of Square Toe Mountain. I am calling about a very critical situation. Please connect me with the Governor. I am certain that he will . . ."

The voice was not as polite as she was. It broke right into what she was saying.

"When you hear the tone," it said, "please leave your name and number. The Governor will get back to you as soon as he can."

"It's an answering machine!" Miss Pickerell muttered furiously.

The voice was talking again.

"Please be sure to wait for the tone before leaving your message," it warned her.

"I will do no such thing," Miss Pickerell shouted into the telephone. "That is what I want you to tell the Governor."

It was no use. The signal had come and gone. The answering machine had removed itself from the line. And she hadn't left her name at the time that the machine had told her to do this. For a moment she wondered whether she should not call again and follow the machine's instructions. The Governor might call her back and . . .

"No!" she told herself emphatically. "It may be hours before he gets to the machine to listen for his messages. No, I'd better call him on his private number."

Miss Pickerell remembered very well when he had given her this number. "It is for emergency use *only,* my dear Miss Pickerell," he had said. *"Never for anything else!"*

"Well, this is certainly an emergency, if there ever was one," she told herself, as she consulted her list of special numbers in the little book that hung

47

handily on a nail next to the telephone. "I'll tell him what Euphus said about the war between the computers and what Professor Humwhistel said about one computer overriding another and about Sampson and . . ."

The Governor was indeed sympathetic when she gave him her explanation. And when she told him what Professor Humwhistel had said about secrecy and the need for official permission to examine the code, his response was instantaneous.

"Of course I will provide that permission," he told her. "To keep this great state on the map, I will do more than that. I will personally accompany you to the Processing Center, Miss Pickerell. I will stay with you for hours, days, a week, as long as it takes to ferret out the villains. Whether they are machines, as your middle nephew believes, or humans, as Professor Humwhistel seems to think, they must be found and dealt with. Will you be ready, my dear Miss Pickerell, if I pick you up in my helicopter within the hour?"

Miss Pickerell quickly consulted her watch.

"I will be waiting for you on my lawn at precisely 3:30," she said.

She began to add up in her mind the things she had to do before then. Nancy Agatha had to be taken up to the pasture. Pumpkins and Sampson had to be fed. Mr. Kettelson had to be asked whether he could come and take care of the animals while she was away.

"I'll call him first," she decided. "I'll feel easier

48

about everything if I don't have that worry on my mind."

But at the sight of her cow, waiting forlornly in the trailer, Miss Pickerell revised her plan of action.

"I'll run up to the pasture first," she decided. "I can't let poor Nancy Agatha feel so neglected."

The telephone was ringing when Miss Pickerell walked into her kitchen again. It was Mr. Kettelson.

"You needn't concern yourself about the animals," he said. "I will stay on your farm with them as long as is necessary. My assistant will take care of the hardware store. It will give him something to do. Business is even worse than usual. As you know, Miss Pickerell, I try to keep up with the times. But absolutely no one has come in to buy those juice extractors I put into my stock last week. They're supposed to be the very latest thing. Still . . ."

Miss Pickerell had tried a number of times and failed to interrupt Mr. Kettelson. When she finally did, it was to ask him how he knew about her trip.

"From Miss Lemon, I suppose," she sighed.

"Not this time," Mr. Kettelson laughed. "This time it was from Miss Phoebe."

"Miss Phoebe Bunter?" Miss Pickerell gasped. "Our postmistress?"

"Didn't you know," Mr. Kettelson inquired, "that they are computerizing the post office? And that Miss Lemon is teaching Miss Phoebe how to become a telephone operator? She was at the switchboard with Miss Lemon when you spoke to the Gov-

49

ernor. By now, all of Square Toe County knows where and when you are going."

Miss Pickerell was sure of this when her doorbell began to ring. First it was Euphus, coming to say that he should be going to the Processing Center, too, since he was the one who knew about computers.

"It was all my idea, anyway," he added. "And I'm going to tell that to the Governor when he gets here."

Then Euphus's mother showed up, carrying Euphus's toothbrush and pajamas.

"I know he'll talk the Governor into letting him go," she said. "And oh, yes, Lavinia, I've brought you some lunch to take with you. Mr. Rugby stopped by to say you hadn't even touched your Eclipse Special and that eating was something you mustn't forget to do."

Then Rosemary appeared, advising Miss Pickerell that she had come to help her pack.

"We'll use your tan valise," she said. "And I'll pick out the dresses for you to take."

Miss Pickerell said that she could put everything she needed right into her knitting bag, including the cat food cans she wanted to take with her. And she had no intention of dragging any dresses along.

"I have the skirt and blouse that I am wearing," she told her oldest niece. "That will be quite enough. And now I'm going to feed Pumpkins and Sampson."

Professor Humwhistel arrived while she was putting the bowls down on the plastic mat. He put a large brown envelope into her open knitting bag.

"It contains something essential for you to read, Miss Pickerell," he said.

Mrs. Broadribb arrived next. She had brought her second-best bird-watching glasses for Miss Pickerell.

"One never knows when they will come in handy," she said, as she stuffed them on top of Professor Humwhistel's envelope.

Mr. Kettelson, Mrs. Ogelthorpe, and the Mayor all arrived together. Mr. Kettelson began talking to Pumpkins and Sampson immediately.

"I'll take good care of you," he told them. "And of Nancy Agatha, too."

Miss Ogelthorpe ran around with her pencil and notebook, asking Miss Pickerell if she had anything she might want to say about how she felt at this moment. Miss Pickerell did not reply. She was busy checking her knitting bag to make sure she had put in an extra handkerchief and the notes that Euphus had made on the back of the dry cleaning bill.

The Mayor said only that he was proud of her and that he wished he were going, too.

"Unfortunately," he complained, "I do not have anyone to take over my duties while I'm away. The State has cut my budget. It has even gone back on its promise to supply funds for the new schoolyard that we need."

Miss Pickerell did not answer him, either. She

was listening to the whir of the helicopter outside. She stopped only to pick up her umbrella and to kiss Pumpkins and Sampson before running to the door. Sampson, who ran faster, stretched himself across the doorway to keep her from leaving. Pumpkins, still faster, raced after her when she managed to get out of the door. Rosemary picked Pumpkins up and tried to comfort him. Euphus was already on the lawn, shouting up to the Governor in the helicopter. The Governor nodded. Euphus jumped up into the helicopter and looked triumphant.

Outside her door, Miss Pickerell paused once more to remind Mr. Kettelson about talking to Nancy Agatha.

"She gets very lonely when no one talks to her," she cautioned him.

Then she gave her glasses an extra-firm push back on her nose and walked across the lawn to meet the Governor. Shiny top hat in hand, he was coming to escort her to the helicopter and to help her climb aboard.

7

Up on Bald Eagle Mountain

A stocky, dark-haired man with a very angry expression on his face was already seated in the helicopter. Miss Pickerell recognized him as the general manager of the Square Toe City Supermarket. He began arguing with her immediately.

"I do not like this one bit," he said, the minute she sat down next to him. "No, not one little bit!"

"To what exactly are you referring, Mr. Quigley?" Miss Pickerell inquired politely.

"To the fact that I've been practically forced by the Governor to go on this wild goose chase in a helicopter," he said, glaring at her. "And I deeply resent the fact that I seem to be the chief target of your suspicions, Miss Pickerell."

"It is not you I have been speculating about," Miss Pickerell said, glaring right back. "It is your computers. In my opinion, there is something very suspicious about their behavior."

"Your opinion!" Mr. Quigley muttered. *"Your* opinion about computers!"

"I'm the one who knows all about them," Euphus shouted from where he sat in front of Mr. Quigley and in back of the Governor's pilot. "Trust me!"

Miss Pickerell was nearly boiling with fury.

"I will not burden you with Euphus's scientific analysis, Mr. Quigley," she said. "But I will ask you why you did not stop to *think* about what might be happening when the computer began to order those outrageous prices."

"Being suspicious of the prices the computer gives us is not part of my job responsibility," Mr. Quigley answered stiffly.

"Then just what is your responsibility?" Miss Pickerell wanted to know.

"To be sure that the prices coming from the computer are stamped on the items in the store," Mr. Quigley replied. "That is my first and most important responsibility."

"You sound even more like a machine than a computer does," Miss Pickerell said heatedly. "I wouldn't have believed it possible."

She turned to the Governor, sitting on her other side, for his opinion. The Governor said nothing. He was looking straight ahead and nervously brushing his clipped gray moustache with his fingers. Euphus moved away from the pilot to join Miss Pickerell, Mr. Quigley, and the Governor.

"I like being a computer detective," he announced. "It's right up my alley. I can snoop around and act as though I know nothing. But all the time I will be . . ."

"I sincerely hope," Mr. Quigley broke in, "that you do not intend to act like that television detective with the dirty raincoat. I turn the set off whenever those reruns of his come on."

"Turn the set off!" the Governor suddenly exclaimed. "Why, my wife simply adored that series. She wouldn't miss one of his reruns for the world. And I must admit that on the few occasions when I've watched with her, I've found the show thoroughly enjoyable."

"Enjoyable?" Mr. Quigley asked. "Enjoyable when you know from the very beginning who committed the crime?"

"But you don't know how the detective is going to find out," Euphus argued. "That's the swell part. That's the . . ."

Miss Pickerell was barely listening to this controversy. She was concerned with taking Professor Humwhistel's large brown envelope out of her knitting bag. He had written her name in the middle of the envelope and printed the word IMPORTANT right underneath. The word was underlined three times with a red crayon.

"There must be some additional scientific information inside," she told herself, as she unfolded the professor's neatly typed sheet of paper. "Something he forgot to tell me."

But the letter was not at all like that. It was a warning.

WE ALL KNOW THE RISKS YOU TOOK WHEN YOU WENT TO THE FAR SIDE OF THE MOON TO GET SOME MEDICINE FOR PUMP-KINS, the Professor began, AND WHEN YOU WENT UP IN A CREAKING BALLOON AND RODE ACROSS THE STORMY ENGLISH CHANNEL SO THAT YOU COULD TACKLE THE ENERGY CRISIS, AND WHEN . . .

Miss Pickerell skipped the next few lines, which listed her various other adventures. She remembered them only too well.

"And besides," she muttered, "that balloon definitely did *not* creak."

In Professor Humwhistel's second paragraph, he stated that he realized Miss Pickerell never expected any danger when she started out on one of her journeys. He also knew that she never wanted to leave her peaceful farm and her beloved animals.

"Of course I never wanted to leave my farm and my animals," Miss Pickerell exclaimed to herself. "And I certainly did not want to leave them today. But *somebody* has to find out *something* about what's going on!"

She went on to the professor's next paragraph.

I AM VERY MUCH AFRAID THAT THE FORCES ENGINEERING THE COMPUTER PRICE CHANGES MAY STOP AT NOTHING TO KEEP YOU FROM FINDING OUT WHAT IS BEING DONE. AND IF YOU DO FIND OUT,

EFFORTS MAY BE MADE TO KEEP YOU SILENT. PLEASE BE CAREFUL THIS TIME!

YOUR VERY CONCERNED FRIEND,
Adrian A. Humwhistel

Miss Pickerell read this part of the letter with a clenched jaw and a sinking sensation in her stomach. She advised herself to put the professor's opinions aside.

"Pooh!" she whispered, as she drew in a very deep breath; she had heard that this helped to calm a person's nerves. "I'm only going to a computer Processing Center this time. Besides, Professor Humwhistel doesn't always know everything for sure."

She reviewed in her mind some of the things the professor had not known for certain. He didn't know who was changing the computer price codes or why. He didn't even know if anyone was really doing this. And he didn't say that Euphus was absolutely wrong in his idea about the computers warring with each other.

"And," she added, "he definitely doesn't know about any special risks waiting for me in the Processing Center, either. If he did, he would certainly tell me just what they are."

She put the letter back into its envelope, pushed it firmly down into her knitting bag, and took out Mrs. Broadribb's second-best bird-watching glasses. She was asking Euphus what he thought about the idea of focusing these on the small print of the cat can labels, when the Governor's pilot broke in.

"Where to now?" he called. "The directions I have aren't too clear."

"One moment," the Governor called back, as he quickly took a slip of paper out of his breast pocket, where the edge of a carefully folded blue-and-white handkerchief showed. "I have the directions right here. They tell us to go over Square Toe Mountain, then over Pine Ridge Mountain, then up on Bald Eagle Mountain."

"We've done all that, Governor," the pilot announced. "Where do we go from here? What do you say, Mr. Quigley? You should know."

"I've never approached the Center by helicopter," Mr. Quigley replied icily. "The view from a car is very different."

"Well, the trip is certainly faster this way," the pilot answered. "Only a twenty-minute ride and . . ."

"Excuse me," Mr. Quigley interrupted, as he picked up Miss Pickerell's bird-watching glasses and looked long and studiously through them.

"Yes? Yes?" the Governor prompted him. "Do you see anything yet?"

Mr. Quigley shook his head and moved to look in the opposite direction. Then he turned halfway back.

"Right there!" he said finally. "It's the building almost directly ahead of us."

Miss Pickerell snatched the glasses from Mr. Quigley's hands. She peered at the building he was pointing to. It was gray and somber and looked as though it had been carved out of the dark, craggy rocks on which it stood.

"Forevermore!" she breathed. "It's like a fortress, a fortress in a fairy tale, the kind where the evil spirits or giants or whatever they were used to live."

Nobody else said anything. Even Euphus was quiet, as the pilot brought the helicopter to a halt in front of the Processing Center.

8

A Computer Called Homer

Three people waiting at the Center's iron gates began walking down the gravel path toward the helicopter. The one in the middle, Miss Pickerell observed, was an unsmiling young man who walked like a soldier on parade, his eyes fixed straight ahead of him. The young woman at his left looked equally severe. She was extremely thin and wore her dark brown hair tightly coiled into a hard knot at the nape of her neck. A somewhat older man, wearing horn-rimmed glasses, walked on the other side. When he came closer, Miss Pickerell could see that the glasses had exceptionally thick lenses in them.

The unsmiling young man spoke first.

"I am Mr. Crisp," he said, staring now at Miss Pickerell's knitting bag and black umbrella. "I am the Chief Programmer for the supermarket computer network operation and in charge of computer research projects at the Center. Miss Blackstock and

Mr. Skeffington make up my Research and Development Team."

He briefly acknowledged the introductions made by Mr. Quigley and shifted his gaze from Miss Pickerell's knitting bag and umbrella to her left shoe.

"He seems to have a habit of looking at objects instead of at people," Miss Pickerell thought to herself, after she had checked on her shoe and made sure that nothing was wrong with it. "Maybe people who work with computers all day eventually become as strange as their machines."

She was wondering whether Euphus or the Governor or Mr. Quigley had also noticed the odd behavior, and she was making a mental note to ask them about it later, when Mr. Crisp spoke again.

"I have been advised," he said, proceeding directly to the business of the visit, "that you are interested in our computer operations. Please follow me."

He led them back up the gravel path and through the iron gates into a long, low-ceilinged hall. The sounds of whirring disks and spinning tapes reached out from partially opened doors along the way. A fully opened door revealed a large number of video screens filled with words and numbers. Miss Pickerell looked inquiringly at Mr. Crisp. He did not answer. He walked to the end of the corridor, turned right, then right again, and up to a door that he opened with a key.

"This is my office," he said. "Please come in."

Whatever doubts Miss Pickerell had had about Mr. Crisp disappeared the instant she entered the room. Computers in all different shapes and sizes took up every inch of wall space. But each one, she noted approvingly, had been carefully and thoroughly dusted. The large wooden desk in the middle of the room and the two chairs next to it had been rubbed with lemon oil, as well. The brass knocker on a door at the other end of the office was brightly polished, and a couch facing the desk had a tidy summer slipcover on it.

Miss Blackstock escorted Miss Pickerell, Euphus, the Governor, and Mr. Quigley to the couch. Then she joined Mr. Crisp and Mr. Skeffington at the desk. The three of them kept up a whispered conversation as they pointed to some information appearing on one of the lit up computer screens.

"I think that one's talking to another computer," said Euphus, who was perched on the arm of the couch next to Miss Pickerell.

"It's probably working on our store budgets," Mr. Quigley groaned.

The Governor sighed deeply.

"I have one of those to help me with my State budget," he said. "It is not entirely satisfactory. The information it gives me about State expenses is very accurate. But so far, it has not provided any suggestions for reducing those expenses."

He was just getting started on a speech about the problems the State had in meeting its many kinds of expenses, when Mr. Crisp turned to them for their attention.

"I will outline the workings of the computers to you," he said. "I will start with the fundamentals."

Miss Pickerell nodded appreciatively. Euphus looked bored.

"The basic hardware of the computer is made up of what we call integrated chips," Mr. Crisp went on. "These chips process and store the program or data that is fed into the computer by means of the keyboard. Chips are usually square in shape and are made mostly of silicon. Some chips have programs stored permanently on them. Any questions so far?"

He smiled at Miss Pickerell. It was a slight but very friendly smile.

"He's just shy. That's what his trouble is," Miss Pickerell said to herself, as she smiled back and shook her head to indicate she had no questions.

The Governor and Mr. Quigley had nothing to say either. But Euphus stood up indignantly.

"A computer is not just a pile of chips," he called out. "It has a memory and . . ."

"I was coming to that," Mr. Crisp replied. "Actually most computers have two types of chips that make up the computer's memory. RAM chips form a kind of temporary memory. RAM stands for *random-access memory*. RAM is like a blank page. You can fill it with programs and information. But when you turn the computer off, anything in RAM will disappear. The checking out of credit cards is a good example of the use of RAM."

Miss Pickerell commented that personally she did not have a very high opinion of credit cards. The Governor disagreed with her. Mr. Crisp resolved the argument by resuming his explanation.

"Permanent memory," he stated, "is stored on

65

ROM chips. ROM stands for *read-only memory*. ROM chips have information or programs permanently "written" on them. Both RAM and ROM chips make up the computer's internal memory. Information can also be kept on disks or tapes that are stored outside the computer. A disk or tape can be put into the computer's disk or tape drive and the signal given for the transfer of the information to the computer's temporary memory, where it can then be read or processed. For the purpose of comparison of market trends, we like to keep data on our prices and inventories for a long time. That means we have a lot of disks and tapes."

Mr. Crisp paused and looked around. Miss Pickerell sat patiently waiting. The Governor was mopping his brow with his blue-and-white handkerchief. Mr. Quigley was crossing and uncrossing his legs. Euphus was yawning. Miss Pickerell made another mental note, to be sure to talk to Euphus about his manners at the very earliest opportunity. She also gave him a stern warning glance.

"I can't help it," he whispered. "This is old stuff. I want to hear about the *bugs*."

"With a responsible programmer," replied Mr. Crisp, who had heard every word, "there can be no mistakes, or bugs, as you call them."

Miss Pickerell was not at all certain that Mr. Crisp was saying all that needed to be said on that subject. But she did not think that now was the time to discuss it.

"What I would like to know, Mr. Crisp," she

said instead, coming directly to the point, "is whether the bar codes on your merchandise accurately reflect the pricing program in your computer, and if so, how do you justify such prices?"

"I have brought official permission for this investigation," the Governor broke in with stiff authority.

"Ah!" Mr. Skeffington, who so far had not said a word, exclaimed. "Miss Pickerell is interested in Homer!"

"The computer that our pricing program goes out on," Miss Blackstock added.

Mr. Crisp was looking down at Miss Pickerell's shoes again, this time mostly at her right one.

"The program you are referring to," he said, "contains not only the price codes but also information about our stock, the brands and sizes we carry, the profit margins, the . . ."

"I understand all that," the Governor interrupted. "Mr. MacLean, your Board Chairman . . ."

"Not Chairman," Miss Blackstock corrected. "Second Vice-President."

"Thank you," the Governor replied. "In any case, when we spoke earlier in the day, I advised him that I totally respect his desire to keep all that private. I am interested only in the information about the astronomical price changes that are descending upon my great State and that I have promised myself and Miss Pickerell to . . ."

Mr. Crisp had stopped listening. He was glancing uneasily at Miss Blackstock and Mr. Skeffington. Miss Blackstock shrugged her shoulders. Mr. Skeffington had only a blank stare on his face. Mr. Crisp scowled in return.

"Very well, then," he said finally. "Come with me."

They followed him out through the door with the polished brass knocker on it, into another corridor, and then through another door, which he opened again with a key. All that Miss Pickerell could see in this room were glass cabinets. Each cabinet had a big white label pasted on the front. The labels showed different dates and letters of the alphabet next to them.

"This is our Center's memory room—our data bank," Mr. Crisp explained. "The cabinets contain our hard disks and paper files."

"And this is Homer," Miss Blackstock called out proudly, as she pointed to a computer standing on a console in a back corner of the room. "He's very small, but he is a minicomputer, not a micro. They're making computers smaller and smaller these days. And Homer can do just about everything!"

Mr. Crisp wheeled around to look with equal pride at Homer.

"Yes," he agreed. "We can easily check out your price problem on Homer."

"The cans! The cans, Aunt Lavinia!" Euphus hissed. "Give him the cans. They're our EVIDENCE! Remember?"

Miss Pickerell hastily dug a can out of her knitting bag and handed it to Mr. Crisp. He examined the label carefully.

68

"The information about this merchandise is still in the computer," he said, as he quickly began pushing buttons and keys.

The screen lit up with numbers almost immediately. Miss Pickerell, who was in the middle of taking a long breath, almost choked when she saw them.

"There you are, Miss Pickerell," Mr. Crisp said, smiling at her. "The price code is 69 cents, which exactly matches the amount printed on your can."

Miss Blackstock and Mr. Skeffington smiled with him. Mr. Quigley laughed out loud.

"I have not lost my mind, Mr. Quigley," Miss Pickerell said to him immediately, "although for a moment I believed I had when I was in your store yesterday. I have simply given Mr. Crisp the wrong can."

Mr. Quigley came close to choking this time. Miss Pickerell turned calmly to Mr. Crisp.

"This is the can I want you to check," she said, giving him the can of Savory Sonnet. "The other can was the Vegetable Stew that I bought last Wednesday, the one that Pumpkins refused to eat."

Mr. Crisp's mouth flew open when he looked at the label and saw the $1.17 noted on it.

"Impossible!" he exclaimed, nearly shrieking with surprise. "Absolutely impossible! I never put through any such change in prices, and I'm the only one here who could have. I'm the only one who works with Homer's pricing program."

He began pressing keys again. The screen lit up with the $1.17 indicated as the price. Mr. Crisp gasped. Mr. Quigley gulped. Miss Blackstock and Mr. Skeffington stared at both of them. Euphus stared at Miss Pickerell. She remained silent. The Governor was the first to speak.

"So you did not increase the prices, Mr. Crisp!" he said. "But there it is, plain as day: $1.17 per can, exactly the amount Miss Pickerell had to pay *and* adding up to a price increase of 300 percent. I repeat, 300 percent! What do you have to say to that, young man?"

But Mr. Crisp was not saying anything. He couldn't take his eyes off the screen. Miss Blackstock and Mr. Skeffington were watching him in dismay. The Governor was glancing questioningly at Miss Pickerell. She was looking expectantly at Euphus. This was the time for him to say something about the war between the computers. He said nothing. She decided to discuss the matter further with him before bringing it up. But she still did not believe that any person could be so wicked as to . . .

"Can't . . . can't computers make their own mistakes, Mr. Crisp?" she asked hesitantly.

"NEVER!" Miss Blackstock, shouting, replied for him. "A computer has no will of its own. It is a tool designed by experts to acquire, organize, store, process, and retrieve huge amounts of data."

"Robots then!" Miss Pickerell shouted back. "I've read about robots cleaning streets and working on automobiles and . . ."

"Robots are programmed, too." Mr. Crisp, now alert again, screamed to make himself heard above

70

the shouting. "They are programmed to do all the things you are mentioning—and more."

"Right!" Euphus called out, screaming even louder. "But what about artificial intelligence? My science teacher says that the day may come when machines will have artificial intelligence and they will take over and then . . ."

Mr. Crisp shook his head. "It hasn't come yet," he interrupted softly. "As far as I know, mercifully not yet."

9

Who Did It, Homer?

Mr. Skeffington had a very simple solution for the entire problem.

"We can get rid of the faulty program," he said. "We can replace it with one that has the correct computer instructions and forget about the whole thing."

The Governor opened his mouth and shut it with a snap.

"Out of the question!" he declared, when he finally started to speak. "Absolutely out of the question! I wouldn't hear of it."

"It is very possible that this was just a mistake, an accident that may never occur again," Mr. Skeffington suggested.

"Not according to your chief," the Governor bellowed, looking pointedly at Mr. Crisp. "I distinctly remember hearing him say that with a responsible programmer, *'there can be no mistakes.'*"

Mr. Crisp said nothing. The Governor went on talking.

"This is no trivial matter," he said. "This is a violation of our human rights and security. What's more, the tool that enabled this villain to violate the security of a supermarket chain can also enable him or her to violate the security of our nation, to learn the secrets that keep our nation at peace and . . ."

"I saw a movie about that sort of danger," Euphus interrupted. "I saw it with Rosemary. It sure left her scared."

"And well it might," the Governor agreed.

He paused to mop his brow again before continuing. But Miss Blackstock did not wait.

"How do we solve this mystery?" she whispered hoarsely. "Where . . . where do we begin?"

"We begin at the beginning," Miss Pickerell replied promptly. "With the password."

"The password!" Mr. Skeffington exclaimed. "You gave us the impression, Miss Pickerell, that you knew nothing about computers. Where did you . . . ?"

"I may know nothing about computers, Mr. Skeffington," Miss Pickerell retorted sharply. "But I can *read*. And I have been reading in the newspapers about people learning or guessing the password and gaining access to computer information."

"Password?" the Governor asked irritably. "I didn't know about passwords. His Honor, the Mayor, has recently bought a computer. With State funds that I supplied, I may add. When he showed it to me, he did not say anything about a password."

"You don't need a password if you don't care about keeping the information secret," Mr. Crisp said. "We do keep our programs and data secret, and we do have passwords."

"Well, then," Miss Pickerell said. "There it is! Somebody stole your password."

"Impossible!" Mr. Crisp replied. "I read that newspaper article, too, Miss Pickerell. And I proceeded to take the proper precautions. I insert a different password into the computer every day."

"Mr. Skeffington is very good at making those up," Miss Blackstock laughed. "He's given us some wonderfully original ones."

"I've supplied a few good ones, myself," Mr. Crisp added. "I've also discarded a few of Mr. Skeffington's, those that I considered much too ridiculous. I didn't think he'd mind, and . . ."

Miss Pickerell hastened to dismiss the turn that the conversation was taking. "We are getting off the subject," she said briskly. "If there is no question about the password, we must proceed to the next possibility. We need to sit down quietly and *think*."

Mr. Crisp nodded. He led them back to his office.

"I don't need to think about it," Euphus said the minute he sat down. "I know what we can do. We can ask Homer."

"Ask Homer what?" Mr. Quigley wanted to know.

"Ask Homer if he recognized the voice of the person who gave him the wrong instructions," Euphus replied instantly.

Mr. Crisp sighed.

"There are computers that can do that," he said. "But Homer is not capable of voice recognition. He cannot understand spoken language."

"I know!" Euphus shouted. "Optical systems! Pictures can be communicated with the use of optical fibers or lasers. I learned about that in my science class. My teacher said that a computer can accept information from *anything* that can produce electronic symbols that can be converted into computer bits."

"True!" Mr. Skeffington told him. "Absolutely true!"

"But we have not programmed Homer with any pictures," Mr. Crisp added.

"Besides," Miss Blackstock wailed, "the price codes have no pictures on . . ."

"BITS?" the Governor interrupted loudly, after saying "Excuse me" to Miss Blackstock. "Did you say computer bits, Euphus? What may I ask are those?"

"A bunch of them together can represent a letter," Mr. Crisp explained, "a letter of the alphabet. Eight bits make up what we refer to as a byte. It's all part of the machine's language. A program inside the computer translates what we type on the keyboard into this language."

"Indeed!" the Governor commented, smoothing his moustache thoughtfully. "Then there is a computer language."

"There are many computer languages, but computers can really only understand one—machine language. All other languages have to be translated into bits and bytes," Euphus called out. "A string of bytes can be used to make up a complete word, right?"

"Something like that," Mr. Crisp replied. "Homer is a thirty-two bit computer."

"Wow!" Euphus exclaimed. "That means he can do twice as much and go twice as fast as the ordinary sixteen-bit computer."

Mr. Crisp, Miss Blackstock, and Mr. Skeffington all nodded. Mr. Quigley looked annoyed.

"So far, Euphus," he said, "you have demonstrated that you know a great deal about computers. But you have not gotten us one step closer to the solution of the problem."

"Detectives don't work that fast," Euphus said, sounding thoroughly horrified.

"Certainly not," the Governor agreed. "In that television episode I was watching with my wife, it took the detective days before he found even the first clue. And then . . ."

Miss Pickerell was growing more impatient by the minute. All this talk was getting them nowhere. It was also giving her a nervous headache.

"That's one danger Professor Humwhistel did *not* warn me about," she muttered, as she pushed aside two sheets of paper in her knitting bag to make room for the cat food cans she was again trying to cram inside. "And I can't imagine why I forgot to put this recipe that Mrs. Broadribb returned last week back into my recipe file."

"What *are* you talking about?" the Governor asked her.

"My recipe for raspberry tarts," Miss Pickerell answered. "I was wondering why . . ."

"Disaster looms, and all you can think of are raspberry tarts," the Governor said, in an exasperated voice. "I'm surprised at you, Miss Pickerell."

"Perhaps Miss Pickerell is thinking of them as a way to help us solve this mystery," Mr. Skeffington remarked.

"Oh, no!" Miss Pickerell assured him. "What would my raspberry tarts be doing in a computer?"

"Don't say that!" Euphus shouted. "Computers can plan a menu and . . ."

Miss Pickerell asked him please to lower his voice. She was examining the letter from Professor Humwhistel and looking once more at Mrs. Broadribb's bird-watching glasses. And a totally *new* idea was coming into her head.

"Mr. Crisp," she said, interrupting the conversation between him and Euphus about how a computer could write a cookbook. "Mr. Crisp, I would very much like to go back and take another look at what you showed us on Homer's screen."

"You needn't bother to do that," Mr. Crisp replied. "I'll get you some printouts."

He was out of the room and back with some printed copies almost before Miss Pickerell even had a chance to reply.

"I've brought a copy of each," he said as he handed them to Miss Pickerell.

"Each what?" the Governor inquired.

"Each printout," Mr. Crisp explained. "You see, the computer is programmed to prepare a printout, or paper copy, whenever a price change is made. The date of that price change is on the printout. I've brought you the old printout, the one with the 69-cent price for the cat food, and the new printout, with the $1.17 price."

"The printer is a machine attached to the computer," Miss Blackstock whispered to Miss Pickerell. "It makes the printouts for us. Basically it works like a typewriter, except that a computer, not a person, tells it what to do. We carefully file our printouts for reference should something happen to the electronic records."

"I see," Miss Pickerell said, as she adjusted her glasses to study the two paper copies in her hand.

Euphus, the Governor, and Mr. Quigley were examining the copies over Miss Pickerell's shoulder. Mr. Crisp, Miss Blackstock, and Mr. Skeffington were only waiting for her comments.

"It seems to me," she said at last, "that the letters in the word PRICE, next to the $1.17, are very different from the letters in Professor Humwhistel's typewritten note."

"Anything would look different on that old typewriter the professor uses," Euphus told her.

Miss Pickerell agreed that this might be so.

"But," she went on, "I see that the letters on the two printouts are also different. I am not completely certain, but I believe that the letter *C* in the word PRICE on the old printout is more curved than the *C* on the new printout. The letter *I* appears to be longer and darker, too. How many printers do you use when you work with Homer?"

"Only the printer that is part of Homer's equipment," Mr. Crisp replied immediately.

"That's it!" Euphus shouted. "Somebody must have typed a message on another computer and programmed Homer with it."

"I was about to make the same suggestion," the Governor stated. "I recall a case of fingerprinting evidence that came up in the State Court recently. We proceeded to recheck and . . ."

Mr. Crisp's weary sigh cut him short.

"What Euphus has suggested," he said, "is just not possible. Homer can only be programmed from his own keyboard. And that means that these two printouts, which Homer ordered, must *both* come from Homer's printer—and thus they *must* be identical!"

"Well, that's that!" the Governor declared. "It seems that we have no way of proceeding."

Miss Blackstock added her sigh to the one the Governor was now heaving. Mr. Skeffington remarked that it seemed utterly hopeless. Mr. Quigley said that he was inclined to think so, too. Mr. Crisp stared uneasily at Miss Pickerell.

"You do understand, don't you?" he asked. "My explanation, I mean?"

"Not entirely," Miss Pickerell admitted. "But I still think that the letters in the two printouts are not absolutely identical."

"And what do you suggest that we do about that, Miss Pickerell?" Mr. Skeffington asked.

"Well," Miss Pickerell replied, "I certainly do not know everything there is to know about computers. But it seems to me that such a highly efficient machine should at least be able to tell us whether my suspicions about the differences in the letters are correct."

"Type fonts!" Miss Blackstock exclaimed. "Miss Pickerell would like a comparison of the type fonts."

"Type fonts?" Miss Pickerell murmured.

"Just another word for type design," Mr. Skeffington advised her. "I doubt that Homer is quite ready to do that, Miss Pickerell."

"We have been experimenting with programming Homer for pattern recognition," Miss Blackstock burst out. "We have been trying to get him to recognize letters, pictures . . ."

"So far, we have not made much progress," Mr. Skeffington stated quickly.

"I wouldn't say that," Mr. Crisp argued. "He recognized three letters yesterday, I believe."

"Two, not three," Mr. Skeffington insisted. "Two very dark ones. And those were . . ."

Miss Pickerell, who had been watching Euphus draw diagrams of what he called computers of the future and not listening too carefully to the argument, sprang to sudden attention when she heard Mr. Skeffington's last comment. She began rummaging in her knitting bag instantly. She held Mrs. Broadribb's bird-watching glasses in her hands when she looked up again.

"I don't believe I told you, Mr. Crisp," she

81

said, as soon as she was able to find a moment when he was not occupied in disagreeing with Mr. Skeffington, "I don't think I told you that when Mrs. Broadribb returned my raspberry tart recipe, she said that she and her friend Mr. Trilling had been on a bird-watching walk. With the bird-watching glasses, she told me, she was practically able to count the number of feathers on a starling's head. I'm not at all sure that was completely accurate. But I have been wondering whether we couldn't somehow magnify the characters on the printouts and . . ."

"With the high-resolution camera!" Euphus shouted, hastily putting his diagrams aside. "I saw it on a shelf in the other room."

"A camera's findings are not always accurate," Mr. Skeffington objected instantly.

"I couldn't agree more," Miss Pickerell said sadly. "The pictures I've had taken of Nancy Agatha, my cow, are often not a good likeness. And when I have complained to the photographer, he has . . ."

Mr. Crisp, now walking up and down the room, did not wait for her to finish.

"It's an IDEA!" he called out, from where he had stopped for a moment in front of one of the computers. "The enlarged letters may be just what the computer needs. Homer . . ."

"You really must not underestimate the power of a computer," Miss Blackstock broke in to say.

"I don't," Miss Pickerell informed her. "I had great respect for the computer I met on a spaceship once. It was able to turn the ship in another direction all by itself."

"That was a very simple process of following programmed instructions," Mr. Skeffington explained.

Euphus nodded.

"It sure was," he said. "And I bet this verification will be simple, too, if you use that new gadget my science teacher told us about. I don't remember its name. It's used for pattern recognition, I think."

Mr. Crisp hesitated a long time before answering.

"We . . . we are working on what we call a text reader," he said finally. "It's a type of optical character reader. We believe that our text reader will be able to scan a page and in just seconds convert the typewritten characters on the page into the electronic impulses we can store in the computer's memory. When perfected, it should also be able to make a visual analysis of what it sees. In other words, it should be able to tell us something, about *what* it sees."

"All of that is beside the point," Mr. Skeffington jumped up to protest heatedly. "Our text reader is nowhere near ready for either kind of job now. It would be positively criminal if news about what we are doing leaked out. It would be news about something we are not even sure of ourselves."

"I've had very similar experiences," the Governor said, sighing once more. "On two occasions, I . . ."

Mr. Crisp was not listening to either of them.

"It may be able to do the job with the enlarged copy that Miss Pickerell suggested," he repeated, talking more to himself than to anybody else. "If it does, Homer will be able to compare the characters on the two printouts, to determine whether the shapes are the same or different, whether the pressures on them were the same, whether . . ."

He broke off his sentence to look up at Miss Pickerell.

"If I'm right," he went on, "Homer will be able to say YES or NO to the questions I will ask. I am most grateful to you, Miss Pickerell, to you and your *raspberry tarts*. And, oh yes, to those bird-watching glasses, too."

"It's your experiment," Miss Pickerell reminded him, smiling.

"I'll attend to the camera part first," Mr. Crisp replied, as he moved toward the door. "Then I'll work on the text reader and program Homer. It will take a while, I'm afraid. The programming has to be done one step at a time."

"One instruction at a time," Miss Blackstock corrected.

"And I'll . . ." Mr. Crisp began.

The rest of what he was about to say disappeared with him behind the door.

Euphus clapped his hands. Mr. Quigley got up to stretch his legs.

"Myself," he said, "I don't see much point in this. Finding out HOW the computer change was made is not going to tell us WHO did it."

"It's a *clue*," Euphus said, shouting again. "We *have* to *start* with a clue."

"Well, I wish he'd find his clue in a hurry," Mr. Quigley replied. "I'm getting hungry."

10

Miss Pickerell Suspects

"The worst part is the waiting," Miss Pickerell said irritably as she walked up and down the corridor outside the Center's memory room, with Mr. Skeffington at her side. "I never expected Mr. Crisp to be in there so long."

She paused to exhale a deep breath.

"And we don't even know what we're waiting for," she added. "After all, Mr. Crisp was only *hoping* that Homer would be able to tell him anything."

"He did say that the work would take a while," Mr. Skeffington reminded her. "You could have gone with Miss Blackstock when she offered to show you some of our other equipment."

Miss Pickerell did not bother to reply. She had made it perfectly clear to everybody, Mr. Skeffington included, that she wanted to be *right here* when Mr. Crisp came out with the news. If that meant walking up and down behind the door, with just an occasional rest in one of the two chairs that Mr.

Skeffington had brought out of the office, it was fine with her. She simply wished that Mr. Crisp would hurry up a little.

"Or you could have gone with Euphus, the Governor, and Mr. Quigley to the cafeteria," Mr. Skeffington went on. "You must be hungry by now."

Miss Pickerell wondered for an instant why Mr. Skeffington hadn't gone to get himself something to eat. She decided not to ask.

"I have some sandwiches of my own," she said, instead. "My sister-in-law, Euphus's mother, prepared them for me."

"You'd probably prefer to eat sitting down," Mr. Skeffington suggested.

Miss Pickerell agreed. She carefully draped the handle of her umbrella over the arm of a chair and sat down with the knitting bag at her feet. Mr. Skeffington sat down in the chair alongside her.

"This knitting bag is not usually so disorganized," she said to him, as she picked it up and began to grope again among the crowded contents. "Now, where can those sandwiches be?"

She found them under Professor Humwhistel's letter. They were, she was glad to see, carefully wrapped in wax paper. And her sister-in-law had provided salt and pepper shakers and a number of paper napkins as well.

"Six sandwiches!" Miss Pickerell exclaimed when she counted them. "And all with the fresh tomatoes my sister-in-law grows in her garden! Please have one, Mr. Skeffington."

She held the first sandwich out for him to take. Mr. Skeffington, who was holding his glasses on his lap while he rubbed his tired-looking eyes, extended a hand for the sandwich. Miss Pickerell noticed how he fumbled when he did so.

"Why, he's practically blind without his glasses," she breathed. "He was going 'round and 'round in the air when he tried to find the sandwich."

She also observed that two of the fingers on the hand he extended were very crooked.

"No, oh no!" she whispered, as she attempted to ignore the jolt of fear she suddenly felt. "It can't be! It just can't!"

"I beg your pardon," Mr. Skeffington asked politely. "I didn't quite hear what you were saying."

"It was nothing," Miss Pickerell replied, racking her brains for an explanation she could give him and talking as fast as she could. "I was thinking about my oldest niece, Rosemary, and the foolish clothes she chooses to wear."

Actually she was thinking about the daily menus Mr. Rugby typed for his diner. She had told him once that they looked very unprofessional because the letters didn't all match. A few of them were much lighter than the rest. Mr. Rugby had laughed and said, "Nobody but you would ever notice that, Miss Pickerell." He had also explained that some of his fingers were not as strong as the others and that the same was true of the keys on his old typewriting machine.

"See!" Miss Pickerell went on, talking again to Mr. Skeffington, because she did not want him to know that her mind was elsewhere. "See! I'll show you!"

She hastily pulled a ball of red wool and part of a red-and-white knitted sock out of her bag.

"This is what my oldest niece, Rosemary, has asked for," she told him. "Leg warmers of thick, coarse wool that she wants to wear instead of stockings. She wants to wear them now, in the middle of the summer. They're the latest style in all seasons, she says."

Mr. Skeffington smiled. Miss Pickerell began to knit. Her needles clicked furiously, as she went from row to row and thought some more about Mr. Skeffington. With his two crooked fingers, he would undoubtedly have the same problem as Mr. Rugby. The letters he would type would also be uneven. Maybe that's why the two printouts were different! A different person had typed them—one who had crooked fingers!

It was only after she had reached the place in her knitting where she needed to look at the instructions, and was searching for them in her bag, that she realized how silly her ideas were. Professor Humwhistel's letter, now lying on top of the instructions, brought her to her senses.

"The professor uses an even older typewriter," she told herself. "And he suffers from arthritis in three of his fingers. Of course, what he types may not be as beautiful as the typing on a modern machine, but he is careful and everything comes out even."

Then another thought occurred to her. Homer

did not use an ordinary typewriter. He used a keyboard and a printer. It wouldn't matter how a program was typed in. On the printer, everything would come out all even. The differences in the letters on the printouts probably couldn't come from crooked or weak fingers.

"I'm so ashamed!" she sighed, as she put Rosemary's leg warmers back into the bag. "I think maybe I should apologize to Mr. Skeffington."

But Mr. Skeffington did not look as though he expected any apologies. He had finished his sandwich and replaced the glasses on his nose with great care. Now, he was walking up and down the corridor again and waving cheerily every time he passed her.

"Unless he can read minds," Miss Pickerell assured herself, "he doesn't even know I had those ugly suspicions about him. And besides, in every mystery story I've ever heard of, the detective always has to eliminate some false suspects before he gets to the real one. That's true of Euphus's television detective, too, I'm sure."

She stuffed Professor Humwhistel's letter happily into a corner of her knitting bag and decided that she would join Mr. Skeffington in his pacing. The scissors she kept in the bag fell out as she got up. Mr. Skeffington ran to pick them up.

"They are sharp, aren't they?" he remarked as he replaced them for her, right on top in the bag.

Miss Pickerell was about to tell him why knitting scissors had to be sharp when Miss Blackstock walked into the corridor. She looked at Miss Pickerell's unopened sandwiches lying on her chair and asked what was wrong with them. Miss Pickerell had no time to reply. Euphus, still eating a chocolate-covered jelly doughnut, came bouncing toward her. The Governor and Mr. Quigley followed him. The Governor was saying that his spinach pie had been particularly delicious. Mr. Quigley argued that he had tasted the spinach pie on previous visits to the cafeteria, and that personally he preferred the fish cakes with the spaghetti sauce. He commented too that Mr. Skeffington, who had a number of his meals in the cafeteria, would undoubtedly agree. Mr. Skeffington did not even hear the comment. He was concentrating his entire attention, Miss Pickerell noticed, on the door of the computer room. He was the first to rush forward when Mr. Crisp opened the door and motioned for them to come in.

11

On the Villain's Trail

Miss Pickerell saw, when she walked in, that Mr. Crisp had made a few changes in the room. Homer was still standing on his console in the corner of the room. But on the wall next to the computer, Mr. Crisp had hung a large white screen. It was the kind that people used when they wanted to show off their photography slides. Mr. Trilling, she remembered, invited people to come and see his slides whenever he returned from a vacation. He always felt very hurt when his guests did not say that they envied him because he had seen so many wonderful things.

The screen in this room did not have any such interesting pictures on it. When Mr. Crisp led them closer, she could observe that two lines of oversized letters and numbers stretched across it.

"You were right, Miss Pickerell," Mr. Crisp told her immediately. "Blowing up the printouts enabled the computer to see the very small variations that the naked eye does not usually detect. There *must* have been two printers. You will notice, for example, the little tail on the letter *R* in the copy made by the second printer."

"It looks almost like a scripted or written *R,*" Miss Blackstock remarked. "And some of the other letters—they seem a little uneven to me."

Miss Pickerell stole an instant look at Mr. Skeffington.

"An uneven quality?" she asked. "Just what does that mean, Mr. Crisp?"

"Nothing special," Mr. Crisp informed her. "That sort of thing can happen when a printwheel is wearing out."

Miss Pickerell heaved an especially deep sigh of relief.

"In any case," Mr. Crisp went on, "after hooking up the text reader to Homer, I proceeded to take four careful steps."

"Four!" Miss Pickerell exclaimed.

"Four," Mr. Crisp repeated. "The first was to program Homer to give YES and NO answers to the questions fed into the computer for the recognition tests. Here are the results."

He gave a number of printouts to Euphus to pass along.

"Homer recognized the typeface from its own printer," Mr. Crisp continued. "He did not recognize the other. In every case, for each letter and number that came from the second printout, his answer was NO, I DO NOT RECOGNIZE THIS."

"Mercy!" Miss Pickerell whispered. "A computer can do all that!"

"My second step," Mr. Crisp went on, "was a checkup of my first."

"Mr. Crisp is *very* thorough," Mr. Skeffington said approvingly.

"What I did this time," Mr. Crisp explained, "was to reprogram Homer and ask him to answer THEY ARE DIFFERENT or THEY ARE NOT DIFFERENT. Then I put a letter from each of the copies into the computer. The answer was THEY ARE DIFFERENT. I did the same with a number from each of the printouts. Again, Homer's response was that they were different."

"*Extremely* thorough," Mr. Skeffington commented this time.

"My third step," Mr. Crisp said very quietly, "was perhaps the most important one. I figured out how the criminal did it."

Euphus was the only one who did not feel too stunned to speak.

"HOW? HOW? HOW?" he shrieked.

"What the criminal evidently did," Mr. Crisp continued, "was to type the program with the price changes on his own computer and to run off a printed copy of the new program on his own printer. The characters on the printwheel of his printer were, as we now know, a little different from ours, and this showed up, as Miss Pickerell was quick to see, on the printout.

Then, in order to override the current pricing codes, he ran his printout through our text reader."

"No!" Mr. Skeffington exclaimed.

"Yes," Mr. Crisp said. "But the criminal made

95

one very serious mistake. He must have used the printout in our file drawer as his guide, and he did not put it back in the drawer. He put his *own* printout there instead. What he certainly did *not expect* was Miss Pickerell's sharp observation. And we have been operating with his false data ever since."

"Forevermore," Miss Pickerell whispered.

"What a horrible thing to do!" Miss Blackstock moaned.

"Very horrible," Mr. Skeffington agreed. "And carried out by someone who had heard about our experimentation, perhaps by that science teacher Euphus told us about. That seems to me a very reasonable suspicion."

"Impossible!" Euphus said instantly.

"In any case," Mr. Skeffington went on, "I would be inclined to say that this villain is a most enterprising individual."

"Not to my way of thinking," the Governor screamed. "In my view this villain is the usual kind of common criminal. No more and no less! And he will get what he . . ."

"What about the next step?" Euphus called out, shouting the Governor down. "You said there were four."

"Yes," Mr. Crisp replied. "As a final step, I placed all the evidence in our combination safe and spoke to the police. The Chief Inspector is on his way. Our guard has been instructed to call me on the intercom as soon as he arrives."

The buzzing on the intercom sounded just as Mr. Crisp was ending his sentence. He moved to the wall on which the system was installed and said, "Ah, yes, Inspector Potter. Send him right in."

Mr. Potter, a red-faced, round little man was not in police uniform. He wore a pair of brown corduroy slacks and a plaid shirt with pink suspenders hanging loosely over the shoulders. He also looked extremely annoyed. Miss Pickerell suspected that he had been interrupted in the middle of his dinner and that he didn't like the idea at all.

"To be perfectly frank," he said to Mr. Crisp, after he had been introduced, "I don't rightly see how we can proceed with the handling of this case. You've told me how you believe the crime was committed. But you don't have a clue as to who . . ."

"Fingerprints!" Euphus shouted. "The fingerprints!"

"Not when the crime is more than a day or so old," Mr. Potter grunted. "Not a chance in a million of finding them."

He took a quick look around the room.

"I'd bet a bundle this place gets a thorough dusting regularly," he complained.

"Daily," Mr. Crisp informed him.

The Chief Inspector mumbled a few inaudible words. He turned to Euphus when he finished.

"I have a lad of my own not much younger than you," he said. "He keeps talking about fingerprints, too. Are you, by any chance, planning to join the police force when you grow up?"

"No, sir," Euphus told him. "I want to be a scientist."

"I don't blame you," the Chief Inspector sighed.

97

"Scientists are much more respected than police officers. Better paid too, probably."

He looked away from Euphus to talk again to Mr. Crisp.

"Well, back to business," he said. "You told me that no one from the outside can possibly enter this room."

"No," Mr. Crisp told him. "There are no windows, no duplicate keys. And the door is locked and double-locked when we leave."

"I don't trust locks," Mr. Potter replied. "When you've been in this business long enough, you learn."

"But there's no sign of a break-in," Miss Blackstock cried. "The lock is in perfect condition."

"And there's no motive," Mr. Quigley called out. "Certainly no one at the Center would have any reason for committing such a crime."

"No one at all," Mr. Skeffington echoed.

"I've said it before and I'll say it again," the Chief Inspector replied. "Criminals have their own reasons *and* their own way of doing things."

"I don't think we have to bother about the lock," Euphus piped up. "What we need to do now is to check with computer stores to find out who owns a printer with the kind of lettering we are looking for. You could do that right away."

"Not very likely," the Chief Inspector grumbled. "There isn't a computer store for miles in any direction. Even if there were, it would hardly be open at this time of night. And I'm not even talking about the problem of matching up the printouts."

Miss Pickerell looked around. Nobody else

seemed to have any ideas. She didn't either. For a moment she wondered whether the computer, which was already capable of doing so many unheard of things, might not have a suggestion of *its* own to make. She decided that this was too silly to mention.

"I almost wish this crime had been committed in Square Toe City," she muttered. "The villain might have talked to an accomplice when the crime was planned, or even afterward. Miss Lemon would have solved the whole thing in no time."

"Did you say something, Miss Pickerell?" the Governor asked.

"Not really," she answered. "Not anything you would want to hear."

"Well," Chief Inspector Potter resumed, "I've written everything you told me over the telephone down in my little book, Mr. Crisp. I'll add what the young boy said about a computer store."

He made a hurried note with a stubby pencil into a notebook that he released from a back pocket.

"But I can't promise you any quick action," he added. "The police have a crowded calendar and . . ."

He dropped both the pencil and the notebook when the protests began. Only Miss Pickerell and the Governor remained quiet. Miss Pickerell couldn't find her voice. The Governor seemed to be trying to swallow.

"I am not entirely unaware of this problem, Chief Inspector," he said, at last. "I have had my own experience with crime victims who have complained to me about delays."

The Chief Inspector said he was glad the Governor knew just how nerve-wracking this could be.

"But this is not the same," Miss Pickerell, only partly in control of her voice, protested. "This is an *enormous* crime that affects the lives of . . ."

"It certainly does," the Governor broke in, his jaw tight now and his eyes blazing. "Miss Pickerell was speaking in behalf of the lives of innocent people and animals. I speak for my great State when I demand that this case be wrapped up *immediately*. A continued business decline will push my budget, which is already teetering, right over the edge. If need be, I will call out the State Guard to act on this crime. I don't believe, Mr. Chief Inspector, that the Police Commissioner would like that at all!"

Chief Inspector Potter returned the Governor's furious glance with one that was both uneasy and astonished.

"I'll be off now," he said gruffly.

"It's too bad . . ." Miss Pickerell began thoughtfully, as Mr. Potter started to walk toward the door.

"What's too bad, Miss Pickerell?" he asked, turning back instantly.

"It's too bad that this crime wasn't committed over the telephone," Miss Pickerell told him. "Miss Lemon could have solved it in no time."

"Miss Lemon!" the Governor exclaimed. "The operator who listens in at the switchboard?"

"It would have been easier to solve with the help of an answering machine, too," Miss Pickerell went on. "The recorded voice could have been recognized and . . ."

"Our computer does keep a record of calls," Miss Blackstock said, interrupting.

"All it does is note the time and duration of the call," Mr. Crisp added. "That's no help. It hardly matters, though. This crime, we know, was not committed over the telephone."

"Well, the lady had a point there," the Chief Inspector said, smiling.

"I was also wondering," Miss Pickerell added, "why the criminal used a different typeface. If he couldn't use Homer, he could at least have used the same brand of printer."

"Maybe he couldn't find one just like it," Euphus suggested.

"Maybe he could and maybe he couldn't," Chief Inspector Potter commented. "Criminals are not always as smart as they think they are. Well, I'll get the boys at the station cracking on this case. And . . ."

He stopped to give the Governor a final glare.

"And I'll be back in the morning," he finished.

"Then I'll stay here *until* the morning," the Governor stated.

"I'd better wait, too," Mr. Quigley said. "Until *something* changes, I have only a store without customers to return to."

Euphus said flatly that he *had* to stay.

"A detective *never* leaves a case in the middle," he declared.

Miss Pickerell called Mr. Kettelson before making up her mind.

"The animals are fine," he told her happily.

"Pumpkins and Sampson have become great friends. They play games all the time. They especially enjoy chasing each other across the pasture."

"What about Nancy Agatha?" Miss Pickerell asked anxiously. "You haven't said anything about her."

"She's in perfect condition," Mr. Kettelson assured her. "She loves watching the others play. Right now she's resting in her barn. When are you coming home, Miss Pickerell? I want to be able to tell her."

"Probably tomorrow," Miss Pickerell said. "I'm staying here for the night. But tell her that I'll surely be back by tomorrow."

12

The House
on the Mountaintop

"Then I'll call the motel and make reservations for all of you," Mr. Crisp said, as he began dialing.

"No, wait!" Miss Blackstock urged. "I don't think Miss Pickerell would like the motel."

"I certainly don't like the appearance of the one on the outskirts of Square Toe City," Miss Pickerell responded immediately. "It has no character. And the noise that comes out of those windows when I pass! Some people never shut off their television sets!"

Euphus laughed. Mr. Skeffington looked properly horrified.

"Ours is probably even worse," he warned her. "Especially at this time of year, with all the tourists. There's also that plumbers' convention in town."

"Cigar makers," Mr. Crisp corrected. "Not plumbers."

"Perhaps Miss Pickerell would prefer to return to her farm," Mr. Skeffington suggested.

"I wouldn't dream of it," Miss Pickerell told him bluntly.

Miss Blackstock walked across the room to put her hand under Miss Pickerell's arm.

"I'll take you home with me," she said. "No, no, you won't be any trouble at all. And we'll be there in no time."

She firmly led Miss Pickerell out of the building and into a car outside.

"I'll drive slowly," she assured her, as she started the engine. "Euphus has already told me you prefer that."

"I never go over thirty-five miles an hour," Miss Pickerell told her.

Miss Blackstock slowed the car with a sudden jerk.

"I didn't realize you meant quite *that* slowly," she murmured.

"Especially when we are going uphill steadily and on a winding road," Miss Pickerell added.

"I understand," Miss Blackstock replied.

Miss Pickerell did not look either to the right or to the left as they proceeded cautiously up the mountain. She kept her eyes practically glued to the speedometer. She transferred them to the road for an instant only when Miss Blackstock was carefully maneuvering the car around still another hairpin curve. Miss Pickerell counted sixteen of them before Miss Blackstock finally brought the car to a stop.

"Here we are, Miss Pickerell," she said. "On the very top of Bald Eagle Mountain."

It was indeed the top, Miss Pickerell observed, with nothing but the deep ravine between them and another mountain on the opposite side.

"That's Pine Ridge Mountain," Miss Blackstock explained. "Mr. Skeffington lives there. He comes to work by cable car. You can see the car where it's partly hidden by the trees."

Miss Pickerell saw the cable car easily. It was painted a bright orange color, and it looked like a long metal box with windows cut out on both sides.

"It connects the two mountaintops," Miss Blackstock explained further. "Mr. Skeffington uses it regularly. Otherwise, he'd have to drive down one mountain and up another and it would take forever. By cable car he can make it in eighteen minutes. And Mr. Skeffington says that he enjoys the scenery. Shall we go inside now?"

Miss Pickerell nodded and followed Miss Blackstock through the shingled front door into the living room. It was spacious and comfortable, with books everywhere and cheerful pillows covering the sofa and easy chairs. Miss Pickerell was not sure that she would have chosen the wallpaper of huge watermelon slices marching horizontally across the room. Herself, if she had wanted a bright fruit pattern, she would have been more disposed toward cherries. She was also certain that Miss Blackstock was not as careful a housekeeper as Mr. Crisp. There was some dust on top of one of the picture frames that Mr. Crisp would never have tolerated.

On the whole, Miss Pickerell decided, she liked Miss Blackstock's house. She was also beginning to like Miss Blackstock. In her own home the young woman seemed to shed the very severe look she wore in the Center. She was casual and friendly and she even giggled when Miss Pickerell told her about Professor Humwhistel and his terrible predictions of disaster.

"In a supermarket Processing Center!" Miss Pickerell exclaimed, laughing too.

She offered to help when Miss Blackstock moved into the kitchen. Miss Blackstock said that she wouldn't hear of it.

"You can sit in the dining room and watch," she suggested. "I'll keep the door to the kitchen open."

She chattered while she leaned in and out of the oven and emptied jars that she took out of the refrigerator. Miss Pickerell did not watch very closely. She was looking out of the broad dining room window at the setting sun and at the sliver of a moon that was beginning to emerge in its place. The chimes of a clock somewhere far away sounded out the hours, and an owl hooted in the distance. Miss Blackstock was just adding napkins to the silver and dishes that were already on the dining room table when Miss Pickerell turned around to say she hadn't realized it was so late.

"Eight o'clock," Miss Blackstock said, checking with her wristwatch and retreating into the kitchen again.

She came back carrying a baked eggplant in its pan on a tray and a basket of hot rolls. Miss Pickerell inhaled the delicious aroma gratefully. The smell of the hot rolls was especially comforting. For the first time that day, she felt really hungry.

Miss Blackstock continued to chatter while she heaped food on Miss Pickerell's plate. She praised the computer's great speed and accuracy and talked about how computer technology was only in its infancy.

"So many new things are happening!" she exclaimed. "Television cameras are being connected to computers. And advances are being made to enable the computer to respond to spoken language. In other words, Miss Pickerell, we will be able to *talk* to computers."

Her voice was especially warm and her eyes glowed when she talked about Mr. Skeffington's interest in computer experimentation.

"He was the one who first thought of how a computer could monitor menus and keep track of what foods are available in the pantry and the refrigerator," she said. "And right now he's thinking of ways in which Homer can be programmed to sense a person's moods and feelings. Then he—Homer I mean—will be able to turn on a phonograph for the right kind of music for a person's mood."

Miss Pickerell could hardly believe this. But she did not think it would be polite to say so.

"Mr. Crisp doesn't seem to have the same interest in experimentation," she said instead, as she thought of how he had dismissed the idea of artificial intelligence.

The severe, guarded look came back on Miss Blackstock's face.

"Mr. Crisp is a very unimaginative person," she said emphatically. "He is also extremely unfair."

Miss Pickerell sat wondering about this. Mr. Crisp had not seemed at all unfair to her. There was most probably another, far more important, reason for Miss Blackstock's low opinion of him.

But Miss Pickerell was feeling far too comfortable to want to pursue any further mysteries. She was feeling so very relaxed that she had to stifle some yawns when Miss Blackstock cleared the table and brought out the tea and a jar of clover honey. Her head was actually drooping by the time she finished drinking her tea. She was greatly relieved when Miss Blackstock said the dishes could wait until morning and showed her where the guest bedroom was.

13

Miss Pickerell
Takes a Chance

"My, oh my, oh my!" Miss Pickerell whispered to herself, as she peered out of the guest bedroom window the next morning. "How beautiful it all is!"

The sun, slanting through the tangled beech and pine trees that she had barely noticed the night before, was shining everywhere. The outline of the mountain across the ravine glowed with it. Even the steep, forbidding rocks that she could see on the sides and across the mountaintop seemed a little less frightening.

"Only good things can happen on a day like this," she told herself cheerfully. "Chief Inspector Potter may even have called with some news. Perhaps Miss Blackstock is only waiting for me to come into the kitchen so that she can tell me."

But Miss Blackstock had nothing to say. Neither did Mr. Skeffington, who was sitting on a kitchen stool, watching her brew coffee. He got up politely when Miss Pickerell entered.

111

"Miss Blackstock has probably told you," he said, "that I sometimes stop in on my way to work."

Miss Blackstock hadn't said any such thing, Miss Pickerell recalled. But Mr. Skeffington's comings and goings were certainly no business of hers. At the moment she felt sorry for the poor man. He looked so very tired and upset. He smiled when he observed her concern.

"I have been up most of the night," he explained while Miss Blackstock was leading him and Miss Pickerell over to the dining room table. "I wanted to get some action going in the local police station."

He paused for a bite of the buttered toast that Miss Blackstock had put on a plate near his coffee cup.

"They're a slow, bumbling lot," he exploded, when he finished chewing and swallowing. "Each and every one of them. And that Potter man heads the list."

Miss Pickerell was a little surprised. Chief Inspector Potter had given her the impression, after the Governor spoke to him, that he was going to act with the utmost speed.

"I gave him up as a lost cause, finally," Mr. Skeffington continued. "I went to the police on *my* side of the ravine."

"Forevermore!" Miss Pickerell exclaimed.

"They know how to *move,"* Mr. Skeffington said, with a distinct grunt of satisfaction. "They made up a plan of action right then and there, while I was sitting with them and telling them about my ideas.

112

They even based their plan on the clues I offered. If you would like to hear about some of them, Miss Pickerell, I can . . ."

"Let her eat her breakfast first," Miss Blackstock pleaded.

Miss Pickerell shook her head and put the orange juice glass she was holding down on the table.

"Please go on, Mr. Skeffington," she said. "My breakfast will wait."

Mr. Skeffington breathed a very long sigh. He had given the police so many clues, he commented, he hardly knew where to begin. He had to stop and think.

"Well, I told them about the tobacco stain," he said at last. "The rusty tobacco stain on the computer printout. Nobody else had thought of that as a clue."

Nobody else had noticed it, either, Miss Pickerell reflected, not even Mr. Crisp or Miss Blackstock, who were very experienced in examining printouts.

"The police agree that we need to search for a programmer in the vicinity who is a heavy smoker," Mr. Skeffington continued.

"That shouldn't be too difficult," Miss Blackstock commented. "There aren't that many computer programmers in this part of the state."

"The police have also agreed," Mr. Skeffington added, "that it is important to track down my clue about the double agent."

"THE DOUBLE AGENT!" Miss Pickerell gasped.

"Your nephew, Euphus, would probably know more about that than you do," Mr. Skeffington suggested. "He has heard, I am certain, about the one who recently jumped bail and escaped somewhere. The government is still trying to find him. It wouldn't surprise me one bit to learn that he was involved in this computer crisis."

Miss Pickerell sat dumbfounded. She didn't know whether to laugh or cry. It occurred to her that Mr. Skeffington might be planning to write a spy novel and that he was trying the plot out on her and Miss Blackstock. There was also the more serious possibility that he was trying to *plant false clues*.

"But why on earth would he want to do that?" she asked herself, "unless . . . unless . . ."

She pushed this thought hastily out of her mind. Why would a respected member of a research and development team want to tamper with a supermarket computer price code? It was ridiculous, just as ridiculous as his idea that a double agent would have designs on a supermarket computer. She felt better when she had figured this out for herself. She felt even more relieved when Miss Blackstock, refilling the half-empty cups with more hot coffee, said that she was inclined to agree with Mr. Skeffington.

"He has never been wrong yet," she said to Miss Pickerell. "No matter how foolish some of his ideas may sound, they always turn out to be correct."

But Miss Pickerell's heart sank into her shoes and her head began to whirl when still another doubt crossed her mind. How was Mr. Skeffington able to

114

convince one police department to take on a case that was already being handled by a different police department in a different part of the state altogether? She personally had never heard of such a situation. It was possible, of course, that he had been more forceful than most people when he talked to the police on the other side of the ravine. Or, what was much more likely, he could have telephoned the Governor at the motel and gotten him to arrange for the transfer of the case to the Pine Ridge Mountain Police. She had every intention of questioning Mr. Skeffington about this the minute he finished his last sip of coffee.

Mr. Skeffington gave her no opportunity, however. Coffee cup in hand, he marched to the dining room window.

"That's the headquarters of the police department on my side," he said, lifting the cup and pointing with it across the ravine. "That building with the lamppost in front of it."

Miss Pickerell looked in the direction that he indicated. She could not be sure which building he meant. A whole clump of buildings, most of them painted a kind of yellow-green, stood about a quarter of a mile to the right of the rocks. And she could not, from such a distance, clearly identify any lamppost. She hastened to take Mrs. Broadribb's bird-watching glasses out of her knitting bag.

"I can give you a better view than that," Mr. Skeffington said, smiling. "I'm going back there just as soon as I have another cup of this absolutely

115

delicious coffee. I'll be glad to have you accompany me. The trip may make me a little late for work, but I hardly think that matters very much now. What do you say, Miss Pickerell?"

Miss Pickerell did not answer immediately. She was glancing uneasily at Mr. Skeffington and debating the question. He certainly did not look like anything but the computer expert that he was. And she *did* have a tendency to let her imagination run away with her at times. A personal interview with the Pine Ridge Police Department would clear that part up for her. And surely, he would not be taking her to meet those people if what he had told her about his conversation with them was not...

"Come, come, Miss Pickerell," Mr. Skeffington urged, smiling again. "I don't want to be *too* late for work."

Miss Pickerell did not return the smile. But she went back into the bedroom for her hat and her umbrella.

14

A Perilous Journey

If there was anything that Miss Pickerell detested, it was climbing ladders. They made her dizzy even before she stepped on the very first rung. She had the same feeling when she saw the long iron staircase leading up to the cable car station. But Mr. Skeffington linked her arm in his and helped her make a slow, steady ascent. He also told her why no one else was on the station when they got there and why the cable car stood empty before them.

"This is an off-schedule hour," he said. "The morning rush of people going to work from one mountain to another is over. The city can't afford to keep the cable car running except during morning and evening rush hours."

Miss Pickerell had heard a great deal about money problems from both the Mayor and the Governor. She understood perfectly what Mr. Skeffington was explaining.

"I was able to secure permission to ride the cable car at other times," Mr. Skeffington added, "because I am familiar with its operation. I don't need a paid employee to run it for me."

Miss Pickerell nodded absently. She was busy looking at the cable car and thinking that it reminded her a little of the trolley cars that used to clang up and down the Square Toe City streets before the City Council voted to install buses instead.

"Our old-fashioned trolley cars rode along a track, too," she commented to Mr. Skeffington.

"Did they?" Mr. Skeffington asked.

"Yes," Miss Pickerell told him. "But that track was safely down on the ground. This one is overhead."

Mr. Skeffington laughed. Miss Pickerell didn't think it was a laughing matter.

"This car just hangs in mid-air!" she exclaimed.

There's nothing to be afraid of," Mr. Skeffington assured her as he held the door of the cable car open for her and escorted her to a seat.

The car began to move the instant Mr. Skeffington pushed something that closed the door. Miss Pickerell put her umbrella and knitting bag on the floor at her feet and held on to her seat with both hands. She also kept her eyes shut tight.

"As I told you, Miss Pickerell," Mr. Skeffington, now standing in front of her, repeated, "there's nothing to be afraid of. Not yet, at any rate."

Miss Pickerell looked up with a start. Mr. Skeffington was smiling down at her. But it was not a friendly smile. The corners of his mouth turned up in a mocking jeer, his eyes were cold and hard, and, when he spoke again, his voice was suddenly harsh.

"I've had enough of all this detective stuff," he said. "I . . ."

"Then . . . then . . ." Miss Pickerell breathed.

"Yes," Mr. Skeffington interrupted. "It was I who broke into the computer system. It was easy, much too easy for the measures Mr. Crisp had taken to protect it."

"How . . . how could you?" Miss Pickerell sputtered.

"If you are referring to how I could possibly have wanted to do such a thing," Mr. Skeffington replied calmly, "I can say that I had my reasons, which I will eventually tell you about. If, on the other hand, you are wondering about how I managed the break-in . . ."

He paused while he leaned over, and waved a long, bony finger under her nose.

"You and your raspberry tarts!" he screeched. "That was the password I dreamed up for the day of my planned break-in. I was going to use the telephone. But Mr. Crisp changed the password without telling me. He kept on changing my passwords."

"He was right to," Miss Pickerell murmured.

"It didn't matter," Mr. Skeffington went on. "In fact, it worked better this way. Homer's monitor program would have recorded the call. I used my home computer system to prepare the text. It would have worked perfectly, if I hadn't been so nervous and accidentally put back my copy of the printout instead of Homer's. But then, no one caught me, *no one* until you came along, you with your raspberry tarts and bird-watching glasses, and they looked in the file, and . . ."

He waved his finger again.

"You almost had me, didn't you, Miss Pickerell?" he sneered. "With all your bright ideas about letters that didn't match and typefaces that were different and who knows what else you would have thought of. You with your heart full of pity for all the poor and suffering in this world. And Euphus, that silly, show-off nephew of yours with his . . ."

"Euphus is not silly," Miss Pickerell burst out heatedly.

Mr. Skeffington let out a grim laugh.

"And you might have trapped me at that," he went on. "The police around here are not as inefficient as they sometimes appear. They would have followed up every one of your clues, no matter how unimportant the Chief Inspector considered them. Come to think of it, though, he might not have actually thought they were unimportant. Mr. Potter is especially good at putting on a dumb act."

Miss Pickerell was about to dispute this when Mr. Skeffington began to laugh again.

"But our dear Chief Inspector," he said mockingly, "will find that he can do nothing at all with whatever clues he follows up. And I will be able to go on with my work."

"Your *work?*" Miss Pickerell asked.

121

"My work in disrupting the economy of this country and gaining control of it," Mr. Skeffington replied, smiling proudly. "Square Toe City and Plentibush City were only the first experimental steps. My plan is to have all the state budgets, not only your Governor's, pushed over the edge, as he so correctly described it. And the country's entire economy will collapse before anybody can figure out what is happening."

"But that is *treason,* an act of . . ." Miss Pickerell began.

Mr. Skeffington ignored her. "My agents are everywhere," he said. "They are waiting for my signal to take over, and replace the foolish majority that makes policy in this country with a government led by me. My government will enforce laws that I create, laws that will not allow personal freedoms to interfere with government authority. People in this country will *obey* the laws I create."

"That's DICTATORSHIP," Miss Pickerell began again, "the kind of foreign dictatorship that we . . ."

"I'm American!" Mr. Skeffington shouted. "One hundred percent American. So are my agents, all of them. But it does not matter what you think, Miss Pickerell. It does not matter a bit. Do you want to know why?"

Miss Pickerell did not answer.

"Because," Mr. Skeffington continued, as he carefully inspected his watch, "because in exactly eleven and a half minutes, my dear Miss Pickerell,

122

you will be crashing into those ROCKS you were looking at with me from Miss Blackstock's dining room window. I have reprogrammed this cable car. It will not stop at the little station that I suggested for you to look at across the ravine. No, this car will go right on, straight into . . ."

Miss Pickerell, unable to speak, gestured her question to him.

"Oh, no," he replied, his mouth a broad leer. "I won't be going with you. The parachute I brought along this morning is lying under the seat in front of us. I will leap out just in time."

"You . . . you won't get away with this," Miss Pickerell whispered.

"Oh yes, I will," Mr. Skeffington replied. "I can shave my head, grow a beard, dress like a tramp. Everyone will think that I perished with you, Miss Pickerell, that my body has been broken into un-recognizable bits. And you . . . you will not be there to tell the tale. Look, Miss Pickerell, the rocks are getting nearer and nearer . . ."

Miss Pickerell stared ahead of her. The rocks were unquestionably nearer. The cable car was head-ing directly toward them. And Mr. Skeffington, as he had planned, was leaning down to pick up his parachute. She heard screeching and swearing the very next instant.

"Forevermore!" she breathed, as she moved to his side.

She saw immediately what had happened. The thick-lensed glasses had fallen off when Mr. Skeffington leaned down for his parachute. He was blinking unseeingly and groping desperately for them. It took Miss Pickerell less than a second to decide what she had to do.

"I must, I *must,*" she told herself, as her jaw clenched and her teeth chattered, she bent down to smash the glasses with her umbrella.

It took Mr. Skeffington less than another second to straighten up. He could not see her too clearly, but he could make out where she was standing. He pounced and reached for her throat. Miss Pickerell screamed as loud as she could. She could not scream for very long. Mr. Skeffington had succeeded in encircling her throat. And he was pressing down *hard.*

15

The Battle in the Sky

Miss Pickerell was almost sinking into unconsciousness when she heard the whir of the helicopter. Mr. Skeffington heard it at exactly the same moment. He let go of her while he looked around. Miss Pickerell, trying to shake the muddled feeling out of her head and rubbing the numbed places on her throat to start the circulation going, looked up, too. It was the Governor's helicopter that was approaching, with Mr. Crisp at the controls and the Governor's pilot seated beside him.

Mr. Crisp was waving to her and making signs with his hands. He was raising them up, over and over again, and he was calling out words that she could not hear. The Governor's pilot was repeating the gesture, lifting his arms up from his waist to a position above his head. Miss Pickerell tried the gesture herself to see if she could make some sense out of it.

"The window! The window!" she gasped suddenly. "He wants me to open a window."

Mr. Crisp nodded vigorously when she pointed to one of the windows. Miss Pickerell nodded back. And when she saw the pilot and Mr. Crisp change places, she knew just what he had in mind. He wanted to leap from the helicopter into the cable car so that he could do something to keep it from crashing into the rocks. Miss Pickerell opened a window immediately.

But Mr. Skeffington also understood Mr. Crisp's intention.

"No, you don't," he shouted, as he banged the window down.

Miss Pickerell ran to open another. She had one advantage over Mr. Skeffington. She could see exactly where she was going. He could not. He stumbled as he chased after her, closing each window that she opened. It was never immediately. But it was always a few seconds too late.

"It's hopeless," she panted as she turned away from still another window that Mr. Skeffington had forcefully banged down. "He's too quick for me. And I . . . I haven't got the strength to keep running anymore."

But Mr. Crisp was not giving up. He was creeping up on the landing gear of the helicopter and balancing himself there.

"He's getting ready to spring into the first window I can manage to keep open," Miss Pickerell breathed. "That brave young man is risking his life for me. I *must* go on trying!"

She continued to race from one window to another. Her stomach was beginning to turn somersaults. Following the helicopter as it swerved from one side of the cable car to the other didn't help any, either. Her head was spinning. Once she felt so dizzy that she nearly fell in front of a window she was racing to open. When she steadied herself, she looked up and saw the rocks looming just ahead.

"Mercy!" she whispered, as she closed her eyes and braced herself for what was coming.

She opened them again when she heard the whir of the helicopter getting louder. It was flying right at the cable car. And Mr. Crisp was pointing and shouting new directions to the pilot.

"He knows there's not a moment more to lose," she breathed. "He's decided to crash into the helicopter. He'll get inside through the window that he shatters. Any second now . . ."

She put her hands over her ears so that she would not hear the burst of the collision. Her body was shaking from head to toe. Her chest felt ready to explode. Her legs were collapsing under her. She was sinking to the floor. This time she was certain that she was about to faint.

16

And Euphus Has the Last Word

But Miss Pickerell did not faint. She heard the crash of the helicopter against the window and saw the pieces of wood and glass and plastic that fell every which way. And she watched Mr. Crisp leaping into the cable car and racing to what was evidently the computer-controlled engine.

"It must be that," she murmured, "because we're going backward now."

She was also able to observe what Mr. Crisp, still bending over the engine, could not see. Mr. Skeffington was putting on his parachute and getting ready to jump.

"Yoo hoo! Yoo hoo!" she screeched.

Mr. Skeffington raised his startled eyes for one split second. That was all Miss Pickerell needed to grab her knitting scissors and cut right into one of the parachute straps he was fitting around himself.

"Bravo!" the Governor's pilot called from the

helicopter, which he was flying alongside the broken window.

"A thousand bravos!" Mr. Crisp echoed when he realized what she had done.

Miss Pickerell was too busy talking to Mr. Skeffington to listen.

"You said these scissors were sharp," she reminded him. "And wasn't it nice of you to put them back on *top* in my knitting bag?"

Mr. Skeffington's reply was a muttered curse. Miss Pickerell ignored it. She felt too happy to be bothered by anything Mr. Skeffington could say or do. She leaned out of the window to tell the Governor's pilot how grateful she was for all he had done. And she told Mr. Crisp that he was the bravest man she had ever met. He looked embarrassed and began to concentrate on her shoes again. Miss Pickerell quickly changed the subject.

"How . . . how did you know what was happening?" she asked.

"I suppose it all began with Chief Inspector Potter," he replied. "When he arrived early this morning, he informed us that he had been checking on each member of the research and development team—including myself."

"What?" Miss Pickerell gasped.

"Each of us had access to the computer, Miss Pickerell," Mr. Crisp said. "I suppose he had a right to his suspicions."

"As it turned out . . . " Miss Pickerell began.

"Exactly," Mr. Crisp agreed, "and while he was looking around on Pine Ridge Mountain, he found a printer with a worn-out printwheel buried between a hickory and a pine tree!"

"Mr. Skeffington must have been in a great hurry," Miss Pickerell continued. "Pine Ridge is where he lives. I suppose the Police Inspector knew that."

"I suppose so," Mr. Crisp said. "He sent his police lieutenant to search Mr. Skeffington's house. The lieutenant found a sheet of paper with material of a scientific nature on it *and* the print on the paper matched the print on that second printout."

"Forevermore!" Miss Pickerell breathed.

"And," Mr. Crisp concluded triumphantly, "Miss Blackstock screamed *Mr. Skeffington* the minute she saw the paper this morning."

"She would!!" Mr. Skeffington growled.

"You see, Miss Pickerell," Mr. Crisp went on, "Miss Blackstock recognized the information on the paper. It was some research she had asked Mr. Skeffington to do for her. And right after that she told us that you had just left her house to go out on the cable car with Mr. Skeffington."

Miss Pickerell still did not understand.

"But how did you know," she asked, shuddering at the very memory, "how did you know that he was planning to let me . . ."

She paused. She couldn't even talk about it.

"It was Miss Blackstock's idea," Mr. Crisp said admiringly. "She thought we ought to go see whether he had done anything to the controls in the cable car station because . . ."

Mr. Crisp stopped to throw Mr. Skeffington a contemptuous stare.

"Never mind about him," Miss Pickerell insisted. "You were about to tell me why Miss Blackstock said what she did."

"Because," Mr. Crisp continued, "Mr. Skeffington had once boasted to her about how he could control the cable car's computer. And, of course, when we got to the cable car station, we found that he had blocked the controls there. We were desperate, absolutely desperate, until your nephew had the idea about the helicopter. He's a very remarkable boy, your middle nephew, Miss Pickerell."

Miss Pickerell nodded. They were approaching Bald Eagle Mountain now, and she could see Euphus waving at her. He was also pointing to a helicopter that was following the one with the Governor's pilot in it. She did not take the time to give it more than a passing glance.

Euphus was the first one to run up the stairs to meet her when she got off the cable car. The Governor and Chief Inspector Potter were right behind him.

"I telephoned the Mayor as soon as I saw the cable car coming back, Aunt Lavinia," Euphus said. "I didn't want him to worry."

"How could he have worried when he knew nothing about the cable car?" Miss Pickerell inquired.

"Oh, I telephoned him about that before," Euphus replied. "I told him the whole story."

"Miss Lemon and Miss Phoebe no doubt overheard both conversations," Miss Pickerell sighed.

"I suppose so," Euphus said, looking up at the second helicopter. Miss Pickerell did not look with him. She was watching the Chief Inspector lead the handcuffed Mr. Skeffington out of the cable car.

"He was plotting to overthrow our government," Miss Pickerell called out to the Chief Inspector. "He wanted to become our dictator."

"I thought it might be something like that," the Chief Inspector muttered. "I got the idea when we went through his papers at home."

"With a search warrant, I hope," the Governor whispered.

"We found the names of his gang and a notebook with his plans written out in detail," Chief Inspector Potter continued. "The entire operation was going to be carried out by computer. Square Toe City and Plentibush City were only the beginning."

"And a very successful beginning!" Mr. Skeffington shouted.

"Get going!" the Chief Inspector told him. "Get down those stairs!"

Miss Pickerell sighed as she watched them go.

"We *must* do *something* to improve our safeguarding measures," she commented to the Governor.

"Technology!" Euphus told him. "Technology will do it!"

The Governor stroked his moustache thoughtfully.

"I will mention that in my next television address," he said. "I will talk about the uses of technology for safeguarding computer information. I . . ."

Whatever else he was going to say was interrupted by Miss Blackstock. She was sobbing into the Governor's blue and white handkerchief that she held under her nose and racing up the stairs toward Mr. Crisp at the same time.

"To think that I trusted that despicable Mr. Skeffington," she wailed. "To think that I believed all the terrible things he said about you. I simply haven't been able to stop crying. I'm so ashamed!"

Mr. Crisp put a comforting arm around her shoulders.

"Wow!" Euphus shouted suddenly. "They're here!"

He raced ahead of Miss Pickerell and the Governor, down the iron staircase, and over to where the two helicopters were landing. The Governor's pilot sat cheerfully waiting in the first one. The second helicopter, Miss Pickerell now saw, held just about as many Square Toe passengers as could get in.

Miss Ogelthorpe, notebook in one hand and pencil in the other, jumped out first. Rosemary, carrying Pumpkins in her arms and leading Sampson on a brand new leash, was second. Mrs. Lonigan, smiling as she patted her little dog reassuringly, came next. Mr. Rugby, shouting that he was substituting for Mr. Kettelson, who believed that his place was on the farm with Nancy Agatha, followed. The

Mayor, busy conferring with Euphus, followed Mr. Rugby.

"I know all about everything from Euphus," the Mayor announced. "I am calling the President to recommend that Miss Pickerell receive an award for preserving the democracy of our nation."

"Hurray! Hurray!" everybody screamed. "Hurray for Miss Pickerell!"

Professor Humwhistel was the last one to emerge from the helicopter.

"Ready to come home now, Miss Pickerell?" he asked. "Ready to return from another of your supposedly safe adventures?"

Miss Pickerell looked at her watch.

"Just as soon as I telephone Mr. Kettelson and remind him about getting some more food for Pumpkins and Sampson," she said. "It's early closing time for the market on Tuesday. If he hurries, he can still . . ."

But it was Euphus who had the last word.

"You could have PROGRAMMED the reminder for Mr. Kettelson," he told her. "With a modern computer it would have been so easy!"